A NEW YORK CHRISTMAS

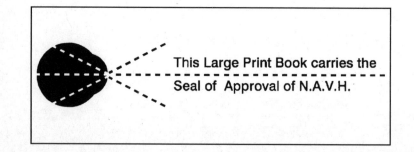

This Large Print Book carries the
Seal of Approval of N.A.V.H.

A New York Christmas

Anne Perry

THORNDIKE PRESS
A part of Gale, Cengage Learning

GALE
CENGAGE Learning·

Farmington Hills, Mich • San Francisco • New York • Waterville, Maine
Meriden, Conn • Mason, Ohio • Chicago

Thorndike Press® Large Print Basic.
The text of this Large Print edition is unabridged.
Other aspects of the book may vary from the original edition.
Set in 19 pt. Plantin.

LIBRARY OF CONGRESS CATALOGING-IN-PUBLICATION DATA

Perry, Anne.
  A New York Christmas / Anne Perry. — Large print edition.
    pages cm. — (Thorndike Press large print basic)
  ISBN 978-1-4104-7341-7 (hardcover) — ISBN 1-4104-7341-4 (hardcover)
    1. Women detectives—Fiction. 2. Murder—Investigation—Fiction. 3. New York (N.Y.)—Fiction. 4. Large type books. 5. Christmas stories. I. Title.
  PR6066.E693N48 2014b
  823'.914—dc23   2014035420

Published in 2014 by arrangement with The Ballantine Publishing Group, a division of Random House LLC, a Penguin Random House Company

Printed in the United States of America
1 2 3 4 5 6 7 18 17 16 15 14

To all the adventurers
of the heart

Jemima stood at the railing on the upper deck of the great ocean liner and gazed across the limitless sea. She had just turned twenty-three and was beginning what promised to be the first real adventure of her life.

It was December 1904, and she was crossing the Atlantic to New York, where she would stay for at least a month. Mr. Edward Cardew had invited her to travel as a companion to his daughter, Delphinia, who was to marry Brent Albright, the son of Rothwell Albright, Mr. Cardew's international business partner. It would be the society wedding of the year.

Phinnie had grown up in London, as Jemima had, but was only nineteen — so it was not at all suitable that she travel alone. Mr. Cardew was an invalid and thus unable to make the journey himself. Someone older and wiser was needed, a person who could be both friend and chaperone. So Jemima had a passage to New York, and an invitation to stay with the Albrights. She had heard that New York was almost as big as London, both raw and sophisticated, a city bursting with life and the expectation of all kinds of new experiences.

If she allowed herself to, Jemima might envy Phinnie her coming marriage, with its promise of happiness shared. Phinnie had met Brent Albright when he visited England the previous year. Within a month she was wildly in love. "He is handsome," she said, as she and Jemima sat together at afternoon tea. "And a great deal more than that. He makes me laugh. He knows about so many things, and yet he is kind. I feel wonderful just thinking of him." She was too discreet to mention that he was also very rich, so would not have courted Phinnie merely for her prospects.

Jemima's prospects were different, although she had to admit that was largely her own fault — or at least her own choice. Like her mother, Charlotte, she wanted adventure, interesting things to do, and, above all, love. She had no wish for a position in society. Perhaps, through tales here and there of her father's experiences and opinions, she had learned too much of its frailties, and she saw even the most powerful of men and the most elegant of women as no less vulnerable to the weaknesses of human nature than the footman or the parlor maid. Her father was Thomas Pitt, head of Special Branch in London. He had begun his career as an ordinary policeman, solving crimes that were often exceedingly grim. Her mother had sometimes helped him in that. Jemima could remember the excitement of it, and the heartbreak. Later, when he was head of Special Branch, his work became more concerned with official government secrets and was much more mysterious, at least to Jemima. That had not prevented Charlotte from participating, something Jemima had always admired about her mother.

In all the planning for this trip, no one had even mentioned Phinnie's mother. One allusion to her a few months ago had made Jemima think she had died when Phinnie was very young, not more than two or three years old. Nothing specific had been said, but the reference had been hurried past in such a manner that she felt it would be clumsy to speak of it again.

Phinnie must have missed her most of her life, but especially now. So Jemima was here to look after her, not only for the sake of propriety but also to be the friend and lookout her mother would have been. It was a trust she vowed to fulfill to the best of her ability. She would not let anything happen to Phinnie.

She smiled to herself, and turned away from the railing, and the wind. *Twenty-three, and I'm thinking like a policeman! You would be proud of me, Papa . . . and horrified!*

Shaking her head, she pulled up the collar of her coat and walked back toward the gangway down to the huge vestibule and the many formal rooms of the liner. She was passed by an elderly woman in a magnificent winter dress. The woman looked her up and down briefly, then nodded an acknowledgment. "Good afternoon, Miss Pitt," she said coolly.

Jemima was surprised that the woman knew her name, and not certain if that was a compliment or not. Then she realized it was actually Phinnie the woman knew. Jemima was merely "the companion." That was not an entirely pleasant thought.

"Good afternoon, Mrs. Weatherby," she replied, lifting her chin a trifle higher, and walking on without waiting to see if there would be a conversation.

She entered the cabin she and Phinnie shared, one of the more luxurious ones on the ship. It had both a bedroom and a quite comfortable-sized sitting room — Phinne was there, curled up in one of the chairs. She was smaller than Jemima and just a trifle plumper, with large, dark eyes — her best features — and thick hair, almost black, with a natural curl that Jemima envied. Jemima's hair was a shining mahogany color, with gleams of amber she did not much like. And it had to be vigorously encouraged to have any curl at all.

Phinnie looked up as Jemima came in. She had just finished writing in her diary, and now she carefully closed it and snapped the tiny lock shut.

"I shall want to remember this," she said with a smile. "I shall not be a single woman much longer. I may forget what it feels like."

"I shall remind you," Jemima replied, closing the door behind her and taking off her coat. She was glad to be in the warmth again. The wind off the ocean had a very sharp edge to it.

Phinnie gave a tiny shrug of one shoulder. "Oh, you may not always be single," she said cheerfully. "You really should turn your attention more fully to the subject. You do not need to be as fortunate as I am in order to be well suited."

A blistering retort rose to Jemima's lips, but she bit it back with difficulty. Phinnie's father was paying her fare, as she had been reminded twice already. She couldn't afford to alienate his daughter.

"Indeed, you are quite right," she said, walking across to the cupboard where she would hang up her coat. She kept her back to Phinnie so the younger woman would not see the expression on her face. "I would be content with far less," she added.

"That is very wise," Phinnie observed approvingly. "To know your own limits is halfway to happiness."

"What is the other half?" Jemima asked, hanging up her coat and turning round. "Knowing your husband's?"

Phinnie was momentarily taken aback.

"Perhaps it is knowing his limits but being careful not to tell him," Jemima said lightly. "Tact is a priceless virtue. It can cover a multitude of misfortunes, don't you think?"

"I don't know," Phinnie said instantly. "I don't have a multitude of misfortunes."

Jemima smiled. "Give it time. You are still very young."

Phinnie's smile vanished. Then with an effort she brought it back a trifle uncertainly. "You say that as if you think something awful is going to happen." There was a tiny whisper of fear in her voice.

Jemima felt guilty. She was having

a wonderful trip at Mr. Cardew's expense, no luxury withheld.

"Of course not," she answered. "Nothing awful is going to happen." But she could not let it go entirely. "However, you would do well to learn a little tact. You are not the only one with feelings."

Phinnie bit her lip. "I'm so sorry. I didn't mean to insult you. I know I'm being selfish. I love Brent so much. I am incredibly fortunate that he loves me too."

"You will never please everybody; no one does," Jemima said more gently. "And it's wonderful that you have Brent. But you also need friends, Phinnie. We all do."

"Not everyone likes you," Phinnie pointed out. "You are very outspo-

ken. Some people say you are opin-
ionated."

"Indeed? And do they mean it as
a compliment?" Jemima inquired
with a slight edge to her voice.

"No, of course they don't."

"Then I am surprised that you
wish to copy me," Jemima rejoined.

Phinnie drew in her breath
sharply and could think of nothing
with which to reply.

Jemima felt victorious, yet she had
no pleasure in it. She went out of
her way to be kinder to Phinnie
that evening and listen to her without interrupting. She managed to
sound impressed when Phinne was
rambling on about the very considerable fortunes made by Albright
and Cardew in their investments,

and their climb from mere respect-
ability to the pinnacle of power and
influence in New York society.

"Everyone is in awe them," Phinnie said with admiration. "Brent
says we shall carry on the family
tradition in all kinds of ways. It will
be marvelous, don't you think?"

Suddenly Phinnie looked cha-
grined, as if she had just realized
that she was speaking of opportuni-
ties Jemima did not have. "I'm
sorry," she said humbly. "I'm being
thoughtless again, aren't I?"

"Not at all," Jemima replied gen-
erously. "In fact, I would love to
hear about the charities they have
endowed. I imagine you will one
day guide some of these charities
yourself."

"Do you think so?" Phinnie said eagerly, the warmth back in her eyes.

Jemima smiled. "I have no doubt."

Phinnie looked down, a slight flush in her cheeks. "As long as I please Brent, that's all I really care about."

That Jemima definitely envied her. She had met a considerable number of young men, and liked many of them well enough, but she had never really been in love. She had felt sparks, and excitement, but it had always been brief, and never accompanied by the deep liking that she had seen between her parents, the kind of friendship that strengthens with time and shared experience. She believed such friendship was the foundation of all the love that mattered.

Perhaps that was why she found it so difficult to meet someone she wished to marry. She could not settle for something that seemed far less than the love she had seen in her own family all her life.

"You'll find someone," Phinnie said with sudden gentleness. "I know it's taking rather long, but don't let that discourage you."

"I won't," Jemima promised, not because it was true but because she did not want to spoil Phinnie's happiness by selfishly indulging in her own feelings. What she meant, and intended to keep, was a promise to herself to look after Phinnie and make this adventure of hers as happy as it could possibly be.

Two days later the ship arrived in New York. From the deck of the liner, the city did not look so very different from London. But as soon as Jemima was ashore she heard the medley of different languages and saw Oriental faces and a good number of black ones, and others that were very fair, as if they were Scandinavian. Everyone was busy. There was an excitement, a tingle in the air, and she fully realized that she had come to a new place, even a new world, and, at least for the moment, alone.

It was overwhelming.

Phinnie clung to Jemima's arm as

people eddied around them. Everyone else seemed to know where they were going.

Jemima felt a moment's panic. Then a slender brown-haired man was standing in front of them.

"Miss Cardew, Miss Pitt? My name is Farrell. I have come to take you home."

He gave orders that their luggage should be brought and conveyed to the carriage that was waiting for them. Discreetly he passed coins to the porters, and their obedience was immediate.

"If you will accompany me," he invited, "we shall go and take our places in the carriage so we may return home, where Mr. Brent is eager to see you."

Phinnie's eyes were bright with anticipation, and her cheeks flushed.

"Oh, yes," she agreed. "That would be very nice. It . . ." She took a deep breath. "It seems like ages since we last met."

"Much too long," Mr. Farrell agreed. "But then the Atlantic is very wide, as I am sure you are acutely aware at this moment. However, you are most welcome." He turned to Jemima. "And you also, Miss Pitt. You will find New York a marvelous city, full of life and adventure, a meeting place for the world." He followed the porter across the open space of the wharf toward the way out, and the road.

"Mr. Albright made sure that all

the necessary paperwork was attended to," Farrell told them. "You will have nothing to do but show it to the officials as we leave."

Phinnie smiled. "I shall thank him. He is so very . . . thoughtful."

"That would be Mr. Rothwell Albright," Farrell corrected her gently. "He is a man of great influence here in New York. But there is no doubt you are already aware of that."

"Oh, yes." Phinnie nodded, covering her error easily. "My father speaks of him often, and with the greatest regard."

Farrell took her arm to help her up the steps, but he did not reply.

Jemima followed after them. Farrell did turn a couple of times to

26

make certain she was not struggling, but the way was easy enough.

The ride from the dockside to the center of Manhattan, where the Albrights had their residence, was so fascinating that Jemima felt no wish to speak at all. Once they were off the main thoroughfare, she saw lots of shop signs not only in foreign languages but in lettering she did not recognize: Russian, perhaps? Or Hebrew? Some were undoubtedly Chinese.

But it was the people who held her attention. At a glance they were much like those of London. She was interested and somewhat comforted to observe the same fashions. At least she would not look as much a foreigner as she felt.

On the narrow pavements groups of young men walked with a little swagger, an air of confidence. They looked around them, surveying their territory, as it were. Was it out of nervousness, or was it the arrogance of those who feel they have destiny in their grasp?

It was too late in the year for open carriages, but there were plenty of horse-drawn vehicles about, especially the wagons of tradesmen. But she also saw more motor vehicles than she could remember having seen in London. Sputtering loudly, they moved at what she judged to be no more than ten miles an hour, not as fast as a good carriage horse.

"It is your first time to New York, Miss Pitt?" Farrell asked her.

Reluctantly she turned to reply. "Yes. I have been to Paris once, but never to America before."

He smiled. "And how do we compare with Paris?"

She smiled back at him. "I think my American will be better than my French," she replied.

He laughed outright. "I have never been outside America, but I hear Paris is marvelous."

"I think this will be marvelous too," she said warmly.

They were passing through a more affluent area now. The buildings were large and handsome, but newer than those she was used to at home, and taller. She counted one on Fifth Avenue that was at least twelve stories high. How odd that such fine streets should have numbers and not names!

They soon arrived at the Albright mansion. Jemima and Phinnie alighted from the carriage, staring for a moment at the gorgeous façade before following Farrell up the steps and into the entrance hall. The chandelier hanging from the high, arched ceiling was the largest Jemima had ever seen. She made an instant decision to be charming, complimentary, and unimpressed. She owed it to her national honor not to gawk as if such things were not common at home.

They were met by Miss Celia Albright, a rather thin lady of uncertain age, who was to be their hostess.

"Welcome, my dear Phinnie," Miss Albright said sweetly. "And to you, Miss Pitt. I hope you will be comfortable here. Mr. Cardew wrote to us to say how kind you had been in offering to accompany Phinnie so she would not have to travel alone." Her face was a trifle too bony to be handsome, and certainly neither her gaunt figure nor her rather ordinary clothes were those of a comely woman. Yet her thick, wavy hair was truly beautiful, and she moved her hands with grace. "I do hope you will enjoy your visit with us."

"I am sure I will," Jemima replied. Phinnie had told her little of Celia Albright, only that she was Mr. Rothwell Albright's unmarried sister. Meeting her, Jemima thought she seemed to lack the confidence that belonging to such a prominent family would confer.

Miss Albright turned again to Phinnie. "May I show you to your rooms? The footman will bring up your cases later. I hope you will find all that you need has been provided."

Phinnie followed Miss Albright up the wide, sweeping staircase. She looked very small behind the older, far taller woman. Jemima, a few steps behind, had the sudden impression that Phinnie was a lost child, far from home, seeking a new safety. It was ridiculous. Phinnie was going to marry a young man who loved her and was offering her a new and wonderful life, filled with every comfort she could wish. It was not as if she were among strangers. The Albrights and the Cardews had been in highly successful business together since long before Phinnie was born. It was almost like a dynastic marriage within an extended family, aristocrats of the financial world.

Jemima was the stranger here, the daughter of a senior policeman but the granddaughter of a gamekeeper, for all that. Her mother was wellborn, but of gentry, certainly not either old wealth or nobility.

But none of that was supposed to matter, here in the New World where all men were equal, where it was the future that was important, not the past.

She drew in a deep breath and followed Phinnie and Miss Albright onto the landing and to the first bedroom, which was to be Phinnie's until the wedding.

When Phinnie was settled, Miss Albright took Jemima to another, smaller room farther along the passage. She opened the door and allowed Jemima to walk in past her.

The room was a surprise. It was dominated not by the charming dressing table but by a window that looked out to the branches of a bare tree. She imagined in the summer it would be gorgeous, but even in the winter its fretwork of dark limbs against the sky was of great beauty.

"I love it!" Jemima said in delight. "It's full of life!" She swung around to face Miss Albright, and was startled to see the emotion in the woman's face. "I know that's silly to say of a leafless tree," she went on, to cover what she thought was a moment of strange, deep sentiment in the other. "But I love bare branches. It is as if the tree is revealing its true self." She tried to think of further explanation, and saw in Miss Albright's face that it was unnecessary.

"I don't know Phinnie very well," Jemima, continued, picking her words carefully, "but I am very close to my own mother, and I cannot imagine how lonely I would be if I were to come to a new country, no matter that they spoke my language, without at least one person I could confide in." She smiled. "Even if it were only to tell them how happy I am, and for them to tell me when I don't look my best, or need advice. This is both a privilege and an adventure for me."

Miss Albright smiled with genuine affection. "I hope it will be both. If you wish to take a short rest before, dinner will be at eight o'clock. Betsy will unpack your cases for you. She is the lady's maid who will be looking after Miss Cardew. We dress formally for dinner, but Betsy will advise you which of your gowns will be the most suitable. I daresay you would like a cup of tea?"

Jemima accepted with gratitude.

■ ■ ■ ■

The dinner was, as Miss Albright had said, very formal for a meal that involved no one outside the family except Jemima. She had accepted the advice of Betsy, who proved to be both efficient and knowledgeable, and had suggested a warm gown of dark green silk velvet with a wide skirt and a most flattering cut at the waist. Jemima was concerned that she might outshine Phinnie, but she need not have been. Phinnie came down the stairs in a gown of apricot silk, which murmured seductively as she walked, the warmth of its shading reflected on her skin, making her seem to glow with happiness.

Or perhaps she really did?

Brent Albright stood at the bottom of the wide staircase, watching her. A little farther back, his older brother, Harley, also waited as suited the occasion.

Harley was slightly taller than Brent, with thick fair hair and a strong face that was not well-enough proportioned to be handsome. Brent, on the other hand, was almost as good-looking as Phinnie had claimed. His hair was darker than Harley's, his eyes a deeper blue. But it was his smile that was most engaging. He held out his hand to Phinnie and she took his arm as she reached the last step, brushing close to him for a moment. Then she lifted her chin and sailed on to be presented to Mr. Rothwell Albright, who stood underneath the magnificent chandelier, the light of it making his silver hair into a kind of halo.

"Welcome to New York, my dear," he said to Phinnie. "I wish your father could be here to join our celebrations, but I understand his reasons for remaining at home. I hope he recovers fully and soon."

"Thank you, sir," Phinnie said modestly. "I am sure he will. The doctors are hopeful."

Mr. Albright turned to Jemima and regarded her with quite open interest. "And you are Miss Jemima Pitt, I believe. I am told by Edward that your father is a policeman of some considerable distinction. Is that true?"

"Yes, sir, it is," Jemima said, and was about to add more, but realized that it was not appropriate at the moment. This evening was in honor of Brent and Phinnie. "I am glad Mr. Cardew spoke so well of him," she added.

"Indeed. I have known Edward for more years than I care to recall. I trust him completely." He offered his arm. "Would you care to accompany me in to dinner, Miss Pitt?"

She accepted his offer and rested her hand on the fine wool cloth of his sleeve as he led the way into the richly decorated dining room.

Miss Celia Albright followed on Harley's arm, and Phinnie on

Brent's.

Though Jemima was determined not to be impressed, she was unable to help it. The room was beautiful, in a way that far surpassed mere showiness. The silver on the table was old and had an elaborate "A" engraved on all the handles. The condiment sets matched. Nothing had the look of being new or unused. Contrary to her preconception, the Albrights clearly had generations of being elite behind them.

"I hope you had a pleasant voyage?" Miss Albright said to Phinnie. "The Atlantic can be a little rough at this time of year."

"Not enough to be uncomfortable, thank you," Phinnie replied.

It had been unpleasant at times, but of course Phinnie knew better than to say so. Jemima wondered if all their conversation was going to be so polite, and generally meaningless. She had a fear that some people's lives were like that: words skimming across the surface of reality, like birds over the waves, without ever getting wet.

"Our voyage to the Bahamas will be quite different," Brent promised with a smile at Phinnie. "We shall bask in the sun, as soon as we are far enough south. Have you ever seen a flying fish?"

Phinnie's eyes opened wide in amazement yet total belief. She would have accepted anything he said. "No, I haven't." She blushed.

"I look forward to that."

Jemima thought for a moment how marvelous it would feel to be so much in love with someone. Then she wondered if she could ever feel that overwhelmed with emotion. Perhaps she was already too old for it, a little too realistic. Or too cynical? That was an ugly thought. After all, how could you find magic if you did not believe in it? She knew people who could look at the most amazing and beautiful things and not see them. She must not turn into someone like that. In a way, such people were the walking dead, passing through life untouched by its joy.

She suddenly realized that Celia Albright was talking to her, and she

43

had not heard what had been said.

"I'm so sorry," she apologized. "I was daydreaming." She should add some explanation. She smiled. "We have been looking forward to this for so long it hardly seems real now that we are here."

Phinnie shot her a smile.

"We will show you some of the sights of New York," Harley Albright offered, and there was no question in his voice. "Miss Cardew will have arrangements to make, and I daresay Celia will accompany her. She knows everyone. Perhaps you would allow me to take you to luncheon at Delmonico's, or the Hotel Astor? A walk in Central Park, if the weather remains clement?"

It seemed like a thoughtful offer, and it would be terrible to be here in this so very vital city and not see as much of it as possible.

"That is most kind of you," Jemima accepted. "I should be delighted." She knew Harley was several years older than Brent, but she had no idea if he worked in the family business or had as much leisure time as he wished. America was different. She had the idea that everyone was always busy, unlike half of London society, but that might be incorrect. "If I am not intruding?" she added, and then wished she had not. The look on his face was gentle but mildly patronizing.

"Not at all, Miss Pitt. You are our

guest, and I should be delighted to show you something of our city, and perhaps a little of our history. There are parts that are very beautiful, others less so, but still of interest. We have just this year opened our subway, which is like your underground railway system. It has twenty-eight stations across town and has made an amazing difference. We really are one city now."

She saw the pride in his eyes, the absolute certainty, and knew that anything but acceptance would be discourteous.

"Then I am very happy to accept," she said cordially.

"We have so many people to meet." Brent took over the conversation, looking at Phinnie as he spoke. "I am looking forward to showing you off to my friends. I don't mean to rush you, but they are all so keen to make your acquaintance, and they are people we shall know for the rest of our lives." He let that observation hang in the air for a moment, so she might take the full meaning of it.

Phinnie lowered her eyes. "I look forward to it."

Jemima knew he was letting her know that all New York high society was to be their social circle, and first impressions mattered.

Miss Albright mentioned a few names, ones that Jemima had heard even in London, or at least read in the court and social columns of *The Times.* Harley added a few more, and Brent continued with details of who was married to whom.

The Albrights were letting them all know exactly where they fit in: at the top of the social hierarchy. It was a welcoming and conversational way of stating their family's position, and their thinly masked pride in it.

Jemima looked occasionally at Phinnie and tried to read her expression. After doing so the third time, she was satisfied that Phinnie was happy and excited, and very little awed by the prospect of living up to such distinction. Her eyes shone with trust as she looked at Brent, and there was a flush of joy in her cheeks. This evening she looked truly beautiful.

Did Jemima envy her? Perhaps.

Did Celia Albright envy her? That was a harder question to answer. Jemima looked across the table and caught the older woman's eye. There was humor in her, and a sadness. Had she ever found anyone she could have loved, and who had been equal to the Albright heritage and pride? Or had she loved and lost someone whose heart she had never touched?

As she sat at this family table, she suddenly felt keenly that she was the only stranger. The world she wanted was far bigger, more dangerous, and perhaps also lonelier. Might she end up like Celia, somewhat on the edge of things? And was it her own naïvety, looking for a love like that between her parents, that put her there?

"Do you have an opinion, Miss Pitt?" Mr. Albright was saying. It had been a political question about Europe and Jemima had caught only the end of it.

"Not yet," she replied with a smile. "I would like to learn a great deal more before I form one."

He looked impressed. "How wise of you," he said approvingly. "I should have known Mr. Cardew would pick a young woman of fine judgment to accompany his daughter on the way to her wedding, since —" He seemed about to add something more, then quite clearly changed his mind; it was obvious from the sudden silence that followed. The thought of Phinnie's mother now hung in the air like a presence.

"Maria would be very proud of you, Phinnie," Celia said gently, breaking the awkwardness and yet somehow making it worse.

Mr. Albright almost smiled at some memory he did not offer to share.

Harley raised his eyebrows, and his voice when he spoke was chilly.

"Maria contributed nothing whatsoever to Phinnie's charm or spirit. They are entirely to Phinnie's own credit, as we all know. Even Maria would not claim to have had anything to do with it."

A dull stain of color marked Celia's face and she struggled for a moment to keep her temper.

"That may be so, Harley," she said. "But truly, any woman would be proud of such a daughter."

Jemima was acutely embarrassed, both for Celia, who had been so publicly criticized, and for Phinnie.

Brent reached out his hand and laid it over Phinnie's on top of the table, where the gesture would not be missed.

"You are about to become part of my family," he said to her, but sufficiently loud for everyone to hear. "You will be mistress of the house, and mother to whatever children we may have. We shall all be proud of you." He looked at Harley, then at Mr. Albright. He did not look at Celia.

Jemima wished she were anywhere else. The reference to Maria Cardew — who, it seemed, was alive after all — had been turned from a passing remark into a painful issue, and poor Celia had been publicly and very sharply reminded that her own place as hostess in the Albright house was about to end. How long she had claimed that status Jemima was not sure. Presumably since Mrs. Albright had died, but she did not know when that was.

Was the title "Aunt" literal, in that she was Mr. Albright's sister, or was the truth that she was some more distant relative, perhaps a cousin? Did she even have another place to go? How many female relatives were used that way, as unpaid servants, and only until someone else took over?

Phinnie looked slightly uncomfortable, but her happiness was too intense to be seriously disturbed by Celia's predicament. "I can think of no greater honor," she said quietly. She turned for a moment to Brent, then away again, as if to ease the emotions that had been aroused and continue with the meal.

Jemima wanted to say something polite and meaningless that they could all grasp on to, but she felt that it was not her place. There was obviously some family issue to do with Maria Cardew that no one wished to address openly yet was always just under the surface. She wondered what it was.

They ate in silence for several minutes. Every touch of knife or fork to the plate was audible. Even the movement of fabric against the padded seats of the chairs could be heard.

"I imagine Christmas will be celebrated wonderfully in New York," Jemima said at length. "It is a time of new beginnings, and so is probably especially appreciated here."

Harley looked at her blankly. "I had always thought of Christmas as a time of tradition above everything else," he remarked. "It is nineteen hundred years old!"

"It is a time of rebirth of hope, and gratitude," she replied, remembering something from a sermon she had heard, under protest, a year ago. "I believe it carries the promise that we can start again, wherever we are." Her look challenged him to argue with her, if he dared refuse the olive branch she held out.

"Of course it is," Mr. Albright said firmly. He smiled very slightly, but with a flash of approval in his eyes, for her tact, and perhaps also for her theology.

"We celebrate it with bells and garlands and music, just as you do," Brent agreed. "And, of course, wonderful food. It is a time for families to be together and rejoice."

That was not what Jemima had meant, but she let it go. They spent the rest of the meal recounting Christmas experiences and traditions that were special to the Albright family. Maria Cardew was not mentioned again, although the late Mrs. Albright was remembered often. It seemed that Harley had been especially close to her, and clearly still missed her presence.

Jemima was sorry that Phinnie would not have an older woman to guide her around the pitfalls of society. She was profoundly grateful for her own mother's advice, and even more for that of her aunt Emily, who was less of a rebel than Charlotte. It was very good to know the rules, even if you did not intend to follow them.

Much later in the evening, when she had already bidden everyone good night and was crossing the upstairs landing on her way to bed, she met Celia Albright.

"Do you have everything you need, Miss Pitt?" Celia asked.

"Oh, yes, thank you," Jemima replied sincerely. "I'm sure I shall sleep very well. You have been most kind."

Celia did not move, as if there were something else she wished to say.

Jemima also hesitated. It would have been a dismissal to have left, and she already felt a sympathy with the older woman, even if it was for a situation she only imagined.

"If you are worried about Phinnie, she may be too excited to sleep, but she is very happy and well suited also," Jemima added.

Celia gave a tiny gesture of resignation. "I'm sure. She will not miss Maria because she never really knew her. A pity, because she was a beautiful woman. Oh, I don't mean her face, although that was lovely too. I mean her courage, her gentleness, her laughter. Whatever else you hear about her, Miss Pitt, don't judge her unkindly. Emotions can run" — she searched for the words — "in ugly paths sometimes. Assumptions are not always correct."

"Assumptions about Mrs. Cardew?"

"I haven't seen her or heard from her in many, many years, but I believe she was a good woman at heart, in spite of appearances."

Celia bit her lip. "Sleep well." She turned away and hurried along the corridor and around the corner, her head high, her thin shoulders stiff.

Jemima went to her own room and closed the door. The curtains were drawn across the window, perhaps to keep out the cold on the glass as much as anything else, but she had liked the sight of the bare trees. It was something familiar and beautiful in a strange new place where she was very much alone.

She thought about Phinnie, madly in love with Brent and on the edge of a new life, with no one but Jemima here by her side. What on earth could have made Maria Cardew leave her only child, little

more than a baby, and surely need-
ing a mother desperately? Jemima
could barely even imagine the loneliness of that child, the bewilder-
ment, the confusion. Why would
any woman do such a thing?

The only thing she was sure of
was that, whatever happened, however much Phinnie irritated her,
she must try harder to be the friend
the girl needed now. She ought
never to feel abandoned again.

For the next three days there were
social events to attend where Phinnie was proudly introduced to some
of the cream of New York society.
There was a soiree with an excellent violinist, and of course the sort
of pleasant conversation Jemima

was used to from parties in London. It was like being on a most elegant stage, everyone acting as if he or she were the star, with polite laughter, sophisticated wit, calculated remarks. Jemima was both disappointed and relieved that it was so familiar, with no hint of adventure to be found. But she could see how well and how easily Phinnie would settle in, and that was all that truly mattered.

The weather was cold but still pleasant, and there were sightseeing trips around Central Park, which was quite attractive, rather different from the London parks. For a start, it was enormous, and far more naturally scenic in spite of being in the very middle of the city.

There were no formal gardens such as Jemima was used to, but some very beautiful walks nonetheless.

There was also a visit to the Metropolitan Opera; very grand indeed, and the music was superb. On the fifth evening there was a ball, and for the first time Jemima was acutely envious of Phinnie. She radiated happiness and had acquired a polish to her beauty that turned more than just Brent Albright's head. Suddenly Jemima ached to have someone look at her the way Brent looked at Phinnie, to feel the safety and warmth of being so loved.

She forced these thoughts from her mind and smiled as if she were enjoying herself. She danced with whoever asked her, even though it was more out of courtesy than desire.

On the following morning, to her surprise, Harley caught up with her as she was crossing the hall to go back up the wide, sweeping staircase to her room.

"Miss Pitt," he said urgently, putting his hand on the carved newel post as if he intended to be there some minutes. "Are you engaged this morning?"

Surely he must know she was not? Celia Albright was taking Phinnie to a dressmaker to have further gowns made for her, with the winter season in mind. She had brought many with her, but one should not appear twice in the same outfit, if in company with people from another recent event. For Phinnie, the only child of a very wealthy man, cost was of no importance at all. Jemima herself had no need of more gowns, and while her family was now financially comfortable, it would remain so only if expenses were regarded with care.

"No," she replied to Harley. "I thought I would take the opportunity to write to my parents and tell them what an exciting city New York is, and that your family has been most kind to me."

"It is our pleasure," he answered, although his smile went no further than his lips. "I'm delighted you find New York so . . . invigorating.

It is my city, and I admit I am proud of it. I would welcome the chance to show you some of the more colorful parts, such as Little Italy. You will be quite safe, and the food is excellent. Of course, it is best explored on foot. Or if you prefer, there is Battery Park, down by the water?"

It was a pleasant idea, and Jemima had no reason to refuse, although she admitted to herself that the invitation surprised her. She believed he made it more from good manners than from a desire for her company. Perhaps his father had suggested he do so.

"Thank you. If you are sure you can spare the time, I would love to see Little Italy. I daresay I may not have the chance again."

"It would be my pleasure," he assured her. "Shall we meet here in half an hour? Please wear your overcoat. The wind is chill."

Harley was quite right. As Jemima sat in the carriage beside him on the way toward Little Italy, the wind was indeed sharp. However, she was too interested in the sights of the bustling streets to mind. He was a good host, explaining the recent history of many of the neighborhoods (including those they would not visit, such as Hell's Kitchen, down by the river).

"Started when they put the tanneries there," he told her. "Made the river filthy, of course, but industry does. Lot of Irish immigrants, fleeing the Great Famine. After the Civil War the population got a whole lot larger, and gang warfare started."

Harley was more talkative than she had expected, and she enjoyed his stories of the city and its different areas. He loved the life, the variety and the courage of the people, and his face grew animated as he spoke. She caught a glimpse of a very different man from the rather stiff one who occupied the mansion. She wondered fleetingly what the arrangement would be when Harley married. He was the older brother, so would Brent then find his own home? Or would they all remain under one roof? The house was certainly large enough.

"This is Little Italy — Mulberry Street, to be exact. Would you like to walk a bit?" Harley invited as the carriage drew to the curb. "Perhaps we could have a hot cup of coffee? There is a place a couple of hundred yards away, not very glamorous, but the coffee is good."

Jemima accepted with pleasure, and fifteen minutes later they were seated in a crowded but most agreeable small restaurant. All around her people were speaking in Italian, a musical language, much of it loud. The walls were hung with pictures of Naples and Sicily, and there were Chianti bottles on the tables.

Harley leaned toward her. "Miss Pitt, may I confide in you? I am certain you have Delphinia's happiness very much at heart, as I have my brother's."

Suddenly she realized why he had brought her here. It was far more than a matter of hospitality, or even of pride in his city. He was deeply concerned about something and it showed clearly now in his face.

"Of course," she agreed, putting her coffee down and giving him her full attention.

He considered a moment before he spoke again, as if carefully formulating his words.

"I am not sure how much Phinnie knows about her mother, Maria Cardew, although that may not be her name now . . ."

Jemima was startled at the mention of Maria's name, especially coming from Harley. She had assumed none of the Albrights wished to speak about her.

Harley saw the expression and smiled bleakly.

"I'm sorry to raise the subject, but you seem by far the best person to turn to. You clearly care for Delphinia and are taking your role in her life most seriously. Your first concern is always her well-being."

Jemima felt herself blushing. He was praising her where she felt she had not yet deserved it sufficiently.

"You are modest," he said quickly. "But what I say is true. Also, if I have understood correctly, your father is a man of some wisdom and experience in matters of . . . I really don't know how to put this delicately . . . of criminal acts . . ." His phrasing was awkward, yet he did not look discomfited. She realized with a rush of very mixed emotions that he was too confident in himself to care what she thought of him.

"He is head of Special Branch," she said coolly. "They are responsible for any threat to the safety of the nation in a criminal or espionage kind of way."

He looked momentarily blank.

"Not military attack," she added for clarification. "Why do you mention my father? Do you think Maria Cardew is a danger to New York?"

This time it was he who blushed,

and a flash of appreciation gleamed in his eyes for an instant.

"No, of course not," he answered. "She is simply a woman of poor judgment and even poorer morals. Despite her being absent for most of Delphinia's life, I am afraid that she may turn up at the wedding. If that happened, it would be in appalling taste and desperately embarrassing. And goodness only knows who she might bring with her. Some of her associates were . . ." He spread his hands in a gesture of hopelessness. "It might be better if I left it to your imagination. I don't wish to use language you would prefer not to hear."

Jemima's imagination was racing. What kind of woman was Maria

Cardew? If she had been impossible to understand before, she was now also frightening.

Jemima could see in her mind's eye the vision of a cathedral wedding, the high-society guests in their gorgeous clothes, with their stiff faces and their polite laughter. And then suddenly Maria Cardew, perhaps drunk, loud-voiced, announcing that she was the mother of the bride. Phinnie would never live it down. Ruin had been brought about by less.

How could any woman twice so injure her own child?

"Is she mad?" she asked quite seriously.

Harley Albright looked at her with something close to gratitude.

"I see that you understand. Yes, I think perhaps she is, and more deserving of our pity than our anger. But the damage she would do to our family, especially Phinnie, who is about to become one of us . . ." He shrugged. "I don't need to describe it. Even the kindest people would find it impossible to forget. The less kind would make it their business to see that no one else ever did!"

Jemima winced at the thought of it.

He misunderstood. "Of course we have enemies, Miss Pitt. It would be dangerously naïve to think that we didn't. We have wealth and power. My father is a generous and good man, but he has been highly successful in business, far more so than some of his acquaintances. My mother was beautiful. That alone can sow the seeds of envy. There are those who would rejoice at our downfall."

Jemima waited for him to continue. She sipped her coffee, but it had lost its flavor.

"That is why I ask you to help me," Harley said gently. "I believe you will, for Phinnie's sake, not mine."

She was puzzled. "What can I do? I can see perfectly how awful it would be if Mrs. Cardew were to turn up at the wedding, but what could any of us do to stop her?" She frowned. "Why do you think she even knows about it?"

"Ah . . ." He let out a sigh. "That is the crux of the whole situation. I am almost certain that she is in New York."

"In New York? That's terrible!" Now she could see the situation perfectly.

"Yes . . . yes it is," he agreed. "I suppose we should have foreseen it. After all, the marriage was announced as the wedding of the year. I imagine that even in other cities it will have been reported in the society columns of newspapers. If Mrs. Cardew read of it, she could be misguided enough to come."

"Surely she must see, after all these years, that she would not be welcome?" Jemima protested. "I don't know the circumstances of her leaving, but nothing alters the fact of it. Phinnie doesn't want to see her. How could she?"

"Exactly." Harley nodded grimly. "I am aware of the circumstances. My mother told me, shortly before she died. But I prefer not to discuss them. Suffice it to say that they could hardly be worse. Will you help me?"

"Of course. But I still don't understand what we can do."

"I have given it a great deal of thought," he replied earnestly. "I can think of nothing else but to find her, and persuade her that she would hurt Phinnie, perhaps irreparably, if she were to appear at the wedding. If she wishes to see her, which I suppose is possible, we could promise to arrange it, but privately." His face registered extreme distaste. "I would even be willing to pay her a certain amount, if she remains several miles away, perhaps even in another city, and never makes the relationship known. I hope that will not be necessary, but as a last resort —"

"Then she could extort money from you indefinitely," Jemima warned. The moment the words were out of her mouth, she wondered if she had been wise to say them.

Harley stared down at the table for several moments before meeting her eyes.

"I had thought of that, Miss Pitt. That is why I hope to persuade her of the unpleasantness of that course. She would earn Delphinia's undying contempt, to say the least. I don't know if it will work. I am unaware of what has become of her and what manner of person she is now."

"And what was she like before?" Jemima asked the question that she knew her father would have asked.

"At the time of her marriage to Cardew?" His eyes widened. "A pretty and ambitious young woman who had already had more than her share of romantic adventures, with all manner of men, but who knew how to please an upper-class Englishman in a foreign country, a man who had no idea such women even existed."

Jemima doubted very much that upper-class Englishmen were anything like as innocent as Harley Albright supposed, but this was not the time to say so.

"I see. Now we are twenty years later, her looks may not be as attractive, nor her health as good," she pointed out.

His face tightened. He looked bleak and even a little frightened.

"Of course. You are quite right. We need to find her, then deal with her in whatever way seems best. I need you to help me, Miss Pitt. You seem to have just the right combination of common sense and imagination, which, coupled with my reputation and my knowledge of New York, should be sufficient."

She nodded. "I will do all that I can. Where shall we start?" New York was a teeming city full of all manner of people; this she knew after barely a week. Maria Cardew could be anywhere, and none of the Albrights had seen her for nearly two decades. She could have changed entirely since then.

"What would your father do?" Harley asked with perfect seriousness.

Pitt would have sent one of his men on the job, but she did not say that. It was certainly not the answer Harley Albright was looking for. She thought hard while the minutes ticked away, and he waited, watching her intently.

She must concentrate her mind,

think logically. Most important of all, she must rescue Phinnie from a ruinous embarrassment. Her future life in New York, and with Brent, would depend upon Maria's not turning up and spoiling it all. Society here would be just like society in London: It would never forget a tragedy, still less a scandal.

Also, in a way, she was representing the intelligence and the standing of her own family.

"She will have found accommodation somewhere," she began thoughtfully. "Either she is staying with a friend, or she has a house or a room. She will be aware that she is not welcome at the Albright home — she will know where it is, but stay out of sight."

Harley nodded but did not interrupt.

"Before we begin to look for her, it would be good to make note of all we know about her. We will have to ask questions of people. The more precise they are, the less time we will waste."

He frowned. "She could be anywhere." His voice held a note of defeat.

"No," she answered, far more firmly than she felt. "There are many areas she will not be, and even among those where she might be, some will be more likely than others. In London I could tell you, but here you will have to think of it."

"What do you mean?" he asked.

"She will need to feel safe." Jemima had tested her ideas in her mind, and hoped she was as reasonable as she sounded. "If there is an area she stayed in before, she might choose it. We all prefer the known to the unknown. It is both easier and pleasanter. Also, she must be able to afford it. Do you know her circumstances? How does she support herself?" The moment the words were out of her mouth she regretted them. The answer was one she could guess, and preferred not to know. But, perhaps in her fifties, Maria had changed her ways. She might well be obliged to.

Harley pursed his lips in an expression of distaste. "She was always good at living off men, one way or another." His voice lifted. "But I see the point of your questions. That does narrow it down considerably. I shall think of them and give you answers. Is there anything else?"

"Yes. What does she look like? Some things don't change much. How tall is she? She may be gray-haired now, but eyes and skin tone do not change so much. What about her voice, her mannerisms? Where might she eat? Is there something she likes that would take her to a particular place?"

"Likes? To eat?" He looked uncertain.

"Yes. When you are far from home, in trouble of any kind, it is natural to turn to something familiar and pleasant. Chocolates? A special kind of tea? A place where you can be alone? A view that has meaning? A particular park to walk in, pictures in a museum, anything?"

He began to smile. "Yes, I see what you mean. You are a credit to your father, Miss Pitt. Would you like another cup of coffee, or shall we return home and begin our quest?"

She rose to her feet. "I think we should begin as soon as possible, Mr. Albright. We cannot afford otherwise."

For the first time in their acquaintance, he smiled at her with genuine warmth.

The next three days were exciting

and of absorbing interest to Jemima. Harley came up with an account of all that he knew about Maria Cardew, which turned out to be a bit more than Jemima had expected.

"She was apparently a very vivacious woman," he began. "Pretty in her own way, and very fashionable. Made herself most agreeable. I think she tried to keep her more eccentric opinions to herself, but she certainly did not always succeed."

"What opinions?" Jemima asked, then saw his expression and wished she had not.

"On racial matters, and people's position in society, property rights. Which is amusing in a dry way, considering she met Edward Cardew in our house, and was quick enough to accept his proposal of marriage."

"Are you saying she was a hypocrite?" Jemima asked as innocently as she could.

"Yes," he said quietly. "I suppose I am. Her subsequent history rather proves my point."

"Yet Miss Albright speaks well of her," Jemima pointed out.

Harley's expression was a mixture of anger and attempted patience.

"Celia likes anyone who likes her, and Maria knew that."

"I see," Jemima replied, forming a strange and not very pleasant picture in her head of a selfish and manipulative woman who had deeply hurt her husband and her only child.

Jemima was careful to say nothing to Phinnie about how she was spending her days. As far as everyone else was concerned, Harley was merely spending time with Jemima in order to show her around the city he knew and loved, and she was greatly enjoying it.

Soon the weather turned much colder. Jemima woke up on the third day of their quest to find everything mantled in white.

"I must show you Central Park in the snow!" Harley said at the breakfast table, a gleam of excitement in his eyes.

"Indeed," Mr. Albright agreed. "It is a wonderful sight. If it is deep

enough, there will be people playing all manner of games. And if
there is ice, there will be skating. I
might come with you . . ."

"Thank you, Father," Harley said
with a very slight drop in his voice.
"But we will be fine. I'm sure you
have matters that need your attention."

Brent stifled a smile; a complete
misunderstanding, as Jemima knew.
Harley had no interest in being
alone in her company. What he had
was an idea as to where they might
find Maria Cardew. Something
about the snow had clearly awak-
ened a memory in him. She could
not afford to pass up this chance.
She bowed her head slightly as if
both happy and self-conscious, and

saw a fleeting look of alarm in Harley's eyes.

"Of course," Mr. Albright agreed, as if he understood perfectly, and it pleased him.

Jemima concentrated on the anticipation of discovering Maria Cardew.

She and Harley set out as early as they could without giving rise to more comment, which she thought he found even more uncomfortable than she did. The air was brisk and the wind had a bite to it, but he did not ask her if she still wished to go out. It would have been the courteous thing to do, even though he knew she would not refuse to go.

They took the carriage as far as

Central Park, then dismissed the driver, saying that their plans were too open for them to estimate a time for him to return. He smiled and drove off.

Harley looked discomfited for a moment, then recovered himself.

"The snow this morning has reminded me of something Aunt Celia once told me, Miss Pitt. Maria Cardew used to enjoy such weather, most especially when the snow was newly fallen and still outlining the branches of the bare trees. If she is here in New York, as I am certain she is, she will be most likely to walk in the park this morning. Of course we could well miss her — it is a very large place — but I do know the best walks for such sights, and undoubtedly Maria does too. If you are willing to go at a brisk pace, we perhaps have a chance of spotting her. Together, we will not draw any unusual attention, and we may follow her to wherever she is staying."

"That is a good plan," she agreed, walking rapidly beside him. "And people will be going carefully, watching that they do not slip, so she will be less likely to notice that the same couple is behind her over a considerable distance."

"Yes," he agreed. "I had not thought of that." He offered her his arm.

She took it as if it was the most natural thing to do.

It was well into the afternoon and

Jemima's feet were aching badly when finally, they spotted a woman of medium height standing on her own some thirty yards ahead of them. She turned to face their direction for a moment, staring up at the light through the snow-laden branches of the trees, her face filled with wonder.

Harley stiffened. His hand grasped Jemima's arm, so she stopped as well. Then, as the woman continued her walk, he moved forward urgently. His pace increased so that gradually the distance between them closed.

"Is that her? Do you want to confront her here?" Jemima asked him breathlessly. "If she makes a scene, we will draw everyone's attention, and if she leaves, we may not be able to follow her to wherever she is lodging."

"I think it is her, but I can't be entirely sure." He let out his breath in annoyance, and slowed down again, allowing the woman in front to reach the edge of the park and walk along the pavement toward a crossing.

The traffic eased and they followed the woman to the other side. She continued along the footpath and they moved a little closer to her so as not to lose her in the general crowd as they went eastward.

"Have you thought what you will say to her?" Jemima asked, but she did not quite hear his reply amid the sounds of the street and the crunch of footsteps in the snow.

Once, she lost Harley in crossing a busy road whose name was merely a number, like most of the ones around them. A wave of panic swept over her. Then she remembered that she had money, she knew the address of the Albright mansion, and she was certainly capable of speaking the language and asking for assistance. There were public conveyances here, just as there were in London. She took a deep breath to calm herself.

The next moment, he was there beside her.

"You had better take my arm, Miss Pitt," he said a little sharply. "It would be disastrous if I were to lose you."

"It would be inconvenient," she corrected him. "I am afraid an elderly lady stepped between us and I could not move around her to keep up with you."

"It can't be helped. I lost the woman, but I am fairly certain it was Maria, and I believe I know the neighborhood where she went. We will go there tomorrow when we have prepared ourselves, and we shall find her exact rooms. Your assistance has been of the highest order, Miss Pitt, and our whole family owes you a considerable debt." He started to walk back the way they had come, automatically taking her with him. "Phinnie will never know of it. I am sure you have more grace and tact than to tell her, but I shall not forget what you have done. I am truly grateful. Now if you are ready, we shall find a cab and return home. It is getting dark, and I think it is very much colder."

Jemima was glad to agree.

Dinner was full of conversation about the wedding: Were they sure the right flowers would be available? Was Aunt Mabel going to recover her health in time to attend? Was the cake perfectly iced yet? Jemima was asked politely about her day, but as soon as she had made clear that it had been enjoyable, and that she was impressed by the beauty of the park in its white covering, discussion returned to the wedding.

She felt a little left out; she didn't know most of the people referred to. But she reminded herself that she was here to look after Phinnie and see that it was truly the happiest day of her life. Above all, without Phinnie ever knowing, she must make certain that Maria Cardew did not get in the way.

She pictured the woman they had seen in the park. Her face, as she turned in wonder to gaze at the snow-mantled trees, had not looked dissipated, or even angry or tired. But Jemima had been some distance away. Closer up, it might have betrayed all kinds of weaknesses, even the beginnings of disease. As her mother was wont to say, "At twenty you have the face nature has given you; at fifty you have the face you deserve." Time has a way of carving your character into you so that all may see it at a glance. The lines of habit cut deep, for better or worse.

The next morning she set out with Harley to find and confront Maria Cardew. He assured her that he had decided exactly what to say to her, and a fall-back attitude to adopt if she should prove unreasonable. He was prepared to offer her money, in spite of Jemima's advice to the contrary.

They were in a coffee shop a block and a half from the building where he suspected Maria had gone on the previous evening when Harley spoke of his plan.

"I am fairly sure I know which building it is, but I don't know which rooms," he told her as they sat opposite each other, their hands around their hot mugs. "I will go and inquire. Perhaps it may be necessary to bribe someone to let me know exactly where she is. Also, of course, I don't know how she is satisfying the landlord regarding her rent," he went on. "It is not a seemly place for you to come, except when I have actually found her. I regret that I have to involve you at all, and I am still hesitant, now that I see the neighborhood in daylight. But I think you may be able to persuade her of the harm she would do Phinnie better than I can. I am ashamed to use your help, but I fear I cannot do without it."

"Mr. Albright," Jemima said urgently, "please don't apologize. We have come this far together, in a cause that is important to both of us. I am not afraid of a slight unpleasantness at the end. Let me know when you find her, and I shall come."

"I admire you, Miss Pitt, and I am most grateful," he replied. Then he ordered another cup of coffee for her, paid for it, and left to go out into the gently falling snow.

A full half hour later, he had still not returned. Wondering what could've kept him, Jemima decided to approach the building herself. If she did not see Harley, she could always return to the coffee shop.

She fastened her coat and went out into the snow. It took her seven or eight minutes walking into the wind before she reached the building. She went in at the entrance and found herself in a tired and rather grubby hall. She understood at once why Harley had not wanted her to come here without him. But what on Earth could've kept him for so long? Jemima walked the length of the hall, annoyed. After a few minutes, she decided it was best that she just return to the coffee shop. As she turned toward the door, a young boy came in.

"Excuse me," Jemima said impulsively. The boy turned toward her and smiled, showing beautiful teeth.

"Do you by chance know which rooms belong to Maria Cardew?" She did not believe he would know, but thought it was worth asking.

The boy nodded. "309, I think," he said, but with so strong an accent from somewhere in Eastern Europe that she took a moment to deduce what he said.

"Thank you!" Jemima gave him a nickel from her purse. He took it and hid it immediately, then gave her another smile and darted outside again.

It was a steep climb to the third floor, but in minutes she was at the top, looking at numbers on the doors. She found 309 at the far end and hesitated outside the door, wondering if she should go down and look for Harley. But perhaps Maria Cardew would be more inclined to listen to her, someone who had no history with the Albright and Cardew families, save being Phinnie's friend? She decided it was worth a try, and knocked on the scratched wooden door.

There was no answer. Actually, it was not completely shut. She gave it a push and it swung wider.

There was a slight rustling sound from inside.

"Mr. Albright?" Jemima called. She would have said "Mrs. Cardew," but she was not certain if that was the name Maria still used!

Again there was no answer, just a faint swish of movement, like the fabric of a long skirt over the floor.

She would have to use some name.

"Mrs. Cardew?" She tried again.

Nothing but the swish of fabric on the floor again. This was absurd. The door was unfastened; there must be someone inside. Jemima pushed the door open the rest of the way and went in, calling again for Mrs. Cardew.

The sitting room was pleasantly furnished but very shabby. One of the windows was open and a curtain blew in the wind, making a slight noise as it moved over the carpet and settled back. That was the sound she had heard.

She stared around her. There were plenty of signs of occupation: a number of books on the shelves, a bag with knitting needles and wool sitting neatly by one of the armchairs, a handmade rug for the knees folded up but within easy reach.

Another door was open and she could see that it led to a tiny kitchen. Anyone inside would have been visible.

"Mrs. Cardew!" she called again, going to the door on the opposite side. She knocked on it and waited, then tried the handle. What could she possibly say in explanation if she intruded into someone's bedroom and found them there? She had no earthly excuse.

And yet she did it.

She saw the woman immediately. The bedroom was small and neat, with two single beds in it. One was neatly made and empty, as if it were not used. On the other a woman lay motionless. The skin of her face was bleached almost gray and her dark hair, streaked with white, was loose and tangled as if she had been moving restlessly only a short while ago. One thin, blue-veined hand rested on the covers.

Jemima felt a shock of grief. She knew the woman was dead, but what struck her most strongly was the difference between this half-sunken face, the life fled from it, and the one she had seen only yesterday, staring up at the snow-laden trees with such joy.

She stood looking at the woman until she heard a sound behind her and swung around, her throat tight with fear.

"Miss Pitt?" Harley's voice broke the trance. "Are you in here? A boy downstairs said he saw you . . ."

Harley appeared and relief overwhelmed her, then vanished again like a huge wave sucking back into itself.

"I think she's dead," she whispered. "Poor soul . . ."

"What!" Harley walked rapidly over to the bed and put his fingers to the skin of the woman's neck. He looked across at Jemima. "Yes, she is, but she is still warm. It can't have been long. Maybe only a few minutes."

She was amazed. "Just a few minutes? If we'd come sooner . . ."

Harley pulled the covers away from the woman's chin and shoulders. Suddenly all Jemima could see was scarlet blood, widespreading, wet, from a heart only just stopped beating. Dizziness overtook her and she had to fight to keep from fainting.

"We had better call the police," Harley said grimly, his voice catching in his throat. "It was not a natural death. She's been stabbed."

Jemima nodded. She tried to speak but no sound came.

"Come," Harley ordered. "There's nothing you can do for her now."

Jemima coughed and cleared her throat. "Is it . . . is it Maria Cardew? She looks so ill!"

"Yes, it's her. Come. We must go and call the police." He held out his hand and obediently she stumbled the few steps to reach him. He gripped her firmly and guided her to the door and out into the passageway. Almost as if it were an afterthought, he pulled the door closed, but she did not hear the latch turn.

They reached the bottom of the stairs and there was no one in sight. Harley went to the front door and out into the street. He looked one way, then the other, then came back to Jemima.

"I'm going to find the nearest

policeman. I don't think anyone around here will have a telephone. It's not that sort of area. You stay here and don't speak to anyone. I'll be back as soon as I can."

"Can't I come with you?" she asked, then heard her own voice and wished she had not sounded so plaintive. No backbone! "No," she said before he could reply, although the refusal was in his face. "Of course not. You'll move far faster without me. I understand. Please go."

He looked immensely relieved and turned quickly, starting to run as soon as he was on the open sidewalk.

Jemima stood in the hallway for what seemed like forever. A man

came out of one of the ground-
floor apartments and said something to her, but she did not hear
the words, could not find her voice
to reply. He went out the door and
disappeared. Two more people went
by.

Her mind was racing.

Who could have killed Maria
Cardew, and why? Had some part
of the evil life Harley had hinted at
finally caught up with her? Where
had Harley been? If he had arrived
sooner, they might have saved her!
Jemima should have felt outrage,
even fear, but thinking of that rav-
aged face all she could summon
was pity. She hoped Phinnie would
not have to learn the whole truth.
Was there any way they could keep

it from her, at least until after the wedding?

She was still busy with that thought when Harley came back in through the front door, followed by a young man easily his height but dark-haired and with startlingly blue eyes. He introduced himself before Harley could do it.

"Miss Pitt? I'm Officer Patrick Flannery. Mr. Albright tells me that you discovered the body of a woman upstairs in apartment 309. Is that true?"

Jemima looked at him. His presence, his dark blue uniform, made it all suddenly no longer a nightmare but a reality — official, ugly, and dangerous. How could they possibly keep Phinnie from knowing? If this young policeman had any brains at all, he would ask what Harley Albright was doing here in the first place. And she knew from her father's experience that lies only made everything worse. He had said more than once that the lies a person told gave away more than most truths.

"Yes, sir," she replied. Another thing her father had said was not to answer more questions than you were asked. It made you appear nervous.

Flannery nodded. "I see. Mr. Albright said that he found you inside the apartment, in the bedroom with the dead woman. Is that right?" He had a nice voice, with a lilt of the Irish in it. "Miss Pitt?" he prompted.

"Yes," she said quickly, trying to keep her composure. Of course Harley had had to say that. She was there already when he arrived. "I didn't touch her," she added, then wished she hadn't. Was she so rattled that she was going to forget all her father's advice already? If only he were here now!

"Mr. Albright says you're English. Is that right?" Flannery asked.

"Yes. I've been here just a few days. I came over for the wedding of a friend."

"I see. That would be Mr. Albright's brother's fiancée?"

Jemima nodded. "Yes, Phinnie — Delphinia — Cardew."

"And do you know the dead

woman, Miss Pitt?"

"No. Mr. Albright says she is Maria Cardew."

Harley stiffened, but he did not interrupt.

"The mother of Mr. Brent Albright's fiancée," Flannery said. "He mentioned that. Perhaps we had better go up to see her. I've sent for the police surgeon to take a look at her." He glanced at Harley.

"The family asks for your discretion and will deeply appreciate it," Harley said. "I will personally pay for a decent burial for the woman."

"Yes, sir." Flannery nodded. "I'll do what I can. If you would lead the way upstairs, please . . . ?"

Harley moved, and Jemima followed him, with Officer Flannery after her. It was then that she realized how much the whole affair had distressed her. She had expected an unpleasant scene, but not death; certainly not violence, blood, then the police. And now there was the fear that she would not be able to protect Phinnie from a grief, or at least a shock, that would deeply overshadow all happiness at the prospect of her upcoming wedding day.

Harley pushed open the apartment door. The latch was broken and had not locked behind them.

"Did you find it like this, sir?" Flannery asked.

"Yes. Miss Pitt was already inside. I told you."

Flannery turned to Jemima, his black eyebrows raised.

Jemima felt a prickle of fear. "Yes. It was open when I pushed it."

"So you went in?"

"Yes."

Flannery looked unhappy. "Did you know Mrs. Cardew?"

"No. But I've known her daughter, Delphinia Cardew, for . . ." It was not so very long, but she must finish the train of thought. "I am here with her for the wedding, to look after her until then. She is only nineteen. Her father is ill and cannot travel. She is . . . estranged from Mrs. Cardew. She has no one else . . . except the Albright family, of course." Was she talking too much and making it even worse?

"So you were trying to bring about a reconciliation with her mother?" Flannery looked dubious. This was plainly at odds with what Harley had implied.

"No. I wished to persuade Mrs. Cardew . . ." She realized with horror what she was about to say, and how it would sound.

"Not to appear at the wedding and cause distress and embarrassment," Harley finished for her.

Flannery shot him a sharp look that was close to dislike, then turned back to Jemima.

"Is that correct, Miss Pitt?" he said gently.

There was no escape.

"Yes." Her voice was hollow, as if she had no air in her lungs. "We hoped she would realize that it would be far better, if she wished to meet with Phinnie again, to do it privately." Should she add that Harley had been willing to pay her not to cause a scandal? No. It sounded desperate.

Flannery nodded, then led the way to the bedroom. The dead woman was lying on the bed exactly as Jemima had left her, the sheet still pulled back to expose the terrible wound. She heard Flannery's sharp intake of breath. He must have seen dead bodies before, but there was something horribly tragic about this elderly woman, so frail-looking, perhaps even dying anyway, who lay alone, soaked in her own blood, her graying hair spread across the pillow, her features etched with pain.

Flannery looked at her closely without touching her, except to place one strong hand briefly on her pulse point. He must have felt that she was still warm. He turned to Jemima, his face filled with pity.

"Did you see any weapon, Miss Pitt? Did you move it?"

"No! Of course not!"

"It would be a natural thing to do."

"My father is a policeman, Officer Flannery. In fact, he is head of Special Branch in England. I know better than to move a weapon from the scene of a death."

He looked grim. "So you know quite a lot about crime?"

Another mistake. "No!" she said hotly. "Only what I have overheard now and then. But if you think about it, it's common sense." She must stop talking, stop telling him too much. She sounded guilty, when really she was only grieved and afraid for Phinnie.

"I see," he acknowledged. He appeared increasingly unhappy. He looked back at Harley. "You said, sir, that you arrived here later than Miss Pitt and found her standing beside the body, which you identified as that of Mrs. Maria Cardew."

"Yes," Harley answered quietly. "I'm sorry, but that is so."

"Where were you, sir?" Flannery met his eyes squarely.

"I didn't see anyone come in

here, if that's what you mean?" Harley replied.

"It's part of what I mean. If you weren't in the street outside, where were you?" Flannery insisted.

"Someone stopped me to ask directions, and I ended up having to take them part of the way," Harley replied a little sharply. "When Miss Pitt wasn't in the coffee shop where I left her, I assumed she must have come here. A boy on the street told me he had seen her, and that she had gone to room 309."

"When did you last see Mrs. Cardew alive, sir?"

"About twenty years ago, when she first met Mr. Cardew. It was through my family that they became acquainted. My father and Mr. Cardew are partners in business."

"Yes, sir, you mentioned that." Flannery's face was pinched, his eyes bleak. It seemed he did not like Harley, for whatever reason. He looked at Jemima again. "Is this all true, Miss Pitt?"

Jemima realized with a chill that made her feel sick exactly how it looked. There was nothing she could deny.

"Yes . . ." she admitted.

Harley spoke before Flannery could. "Miss Pitt, if you moved the knife, however well you meant it, it would be a good thing if you told me. I know your devotion to Miss Cardew, but this is extremely seri-

126

ous. I will do my best to protect you, but really, only the truth will serve now."

He was making it worse, making it sound as if he thought she could have killed the poor woman! Why? It would hardly protect Phinnie. The scandal of having her mother turn up at the wedding would be small compared with that of a murder. Did he really think she was so stupid, so impetuous and hysterical as not to know that? She stared at him, and the answer was clear in the sad, puzzled expression in his eyes.

"I did not touch her!" Her voice sounded frightened, as if she were close to losing control. "I did not touch anything. I didn't even know for certain that she was Maria Cardew."

"Yes, you did," Harley contradicted her. "We saw her in Central Park yesterday evening. We followed her."

"We were fifty yards away!" she protested. "She looks quite different close-up."

"But it is the same woman, Mr. Albright?" Flannery said. "You are quite certain?"

"Yes," Harley said decisively. "There is no doubt. I'm sorry. I . . . I understand your devotion to Phinnie," he said to Jemima. "I believe you did this to protect her. It is my duty to my family now to see that you don't in any way suggest that she had any part in this. I know how intensely she is looking forward to —"

Flannery cut him off with a glance. "If you are looking to protect your family, sir, you would not serve that purpose by suggesting that anyone in your household had a part in this."

A dull color swept up Harley's face, but he did not answer.

Flannery turned to Jemima. "I'm sorry, Miss Pitt, but I have no choice but to take you to the station for further questions."

"But I have no blood on me!" Jemima protested. "I would have . . . if I had done that!" She indicated the body on the bed, but could scarcely look at it.

Flannery swiveled round to look

at the kitchen, where the corner of a wet towel was visible in the sink. He looked back at Jemima.

"Please, Miss Pitt," Flannery said quietly as another policeman came in through the door, followed by a third.

"I'll do what I can," Harley said to Jemima, then turned on his heel and left without looking at Flannery or speaking to him.

The next few hours passed in a daze of misery. Jemima was taken in a closed carriage, her hands manacled together, down to the center of the city, where she was asked questions about her identity, her nationality, and her purpose here in New York. She was finally charged with the murder of Maria Cardew, and her belongings were taken from her, except the clothes she stood up in, and a small handkerchief. She was then placed in a cell and left alone, trembling and queasy with fear and shock.

How could this have happened, in the space of a few hours? It was the middle of the day, yet breakfast time seemed as if it had been in another era. Did Harley really imagine that she had killed Maria Cardew? With a knife from the kitchen? Did he think she was both stupid and cold-blooded enough to have committed murder rather than let Maria make a scene at the wedding?

Why? To protect Phinnie from

embarrassment?

That was absurd, even insane.

Then, sitting on the hard bench that served as a bed, shuddering with cold in the bare, iron-barred cell, she knew the answer. Not to protect Phinnie from embarrassment at all, but to make certain that the wedding went ahead and Phinnie became part of the powerful Albright family, with its immense wealth. Harley had all but hinted as much to Officer Flannery. And then Phinnie would reward her appropriately.

That, of course, had assumed she would not be caught! Now all she would gain was a length of rope to hang her, or whatever they did with murderers in New York!

Would anyone tell her parents? Surely they would?

Then her father would come over and he would find the truth. He had no official status as a policeman, or anything else, here in America, but that would not prevent him. He would do anything to save her. She was not guilty of anything except . . . what? Foolishness? Placing her trust in the wrong person? Overconfidence in her own ability? Perhaps pride? It was a miserable thought.

She was given supper; by then she was hungry enough to eat the rough and tasteless stew. The bed was hard and lumpy and the whole cell was bitterly cold. She slept very badly and woke up so stiff she could not move without pain. And of course there were no clean clothes for her, nothing even to wash in except cold water.

About the middle of the morning, the woman in charge told her that she had a visitor, and to straighten herself up and prepare to be conducted to the room whcrc she could speak to him. She did as she was told, wondering if it would be Harley Albright. What could she say to him? He had practically accused her of killing Maria Cardew in a secret agreement with Phinnie, to save her from any embarrassment in her new life. She hated him for that so much she felt as if she would choke on her words if she even tried to speak to him. He was the one who had asked for her help in finding Maria. And yet, furious as she was, she also knew that he was trying to protect his family. That part she could believe, and even sympathize with.

But when she was conducted to the interview room, her hands again shackled behind her back, it was Mr. Rothwell Albright who stood up from the hard-backed wooden chair, not Harley. He looked tired and so pale it was as if the cold had seeped through everything he wore and reached into his bones. Was it the prospect of scandal that affected him so much?

He looked at her with distress. "Are you all right, Miss Pitt? Unhurt?"

"I am not physically anything worse than stiff and cold, thank you," she replied. She softened her voice. He had at least come to see her. She should be grateful for that. "Would you please contact my father to let him know what has happened to me? I have no way of doing so myself."

"Should it prove necessary, of course I will," he replied. His voice was gravelly, as if he had not slept either.

"It is necessary," she said, with rising panic very nearly breaking through. Had he no idea what was happening? "They have accused me of killing Mrs. Cardew! I didn't even touch her! There was nothing I could do to help her."

"I am afraid it seems otherwise," he answered slowly. "Poor Maria. She did not deserve to die in such a way. She was a good woman . . . misguided, perhaps, but not evil."

There was real grief in his face, in his eyes. It seemed that he did not share Harley's view of Maria, whatever else he felt.

"Mr. Albright, I did not harm her in any way," Jemima said earnestly. "Mr. Harley asked me to help find Maria and persuade her not to attend the wedding and cause embarrassment. That was all I attempted to do. I never saw her at all except for a brief glimpse in the park, and then the next morning when she was dead. I have no idea who hurt her. Please . . . please tell Phinnie that . . ."

He avoided her eyes. "Delphinia
is very distressed. She has now lost
all possibility of reconciliation with
her mother, and this terrible manner of her death has cast a dark
shadow over her forthcoming wedding. I asked her if she wished to
send any message to you, perhaps
of comfort or support. She de-
clined. I'm . . . sorry."

It was another blow. Maybe she
should have expected it. Phinnie
was as changeable as the spring
weather at home. But this hurt.
Surely Phinnie knew her better
than to imagine she would have
killed anyone, let alone a frail old
woman she had never even met?

But of course Phinnie would not

be thinking, only grieving, and fearing that the scandal of murder would affect the Albright family, and spoil the longed-for wedding to Brent.

"I shall contact the best lawyer I can afford, Miss Pitt, and perhaps this matter may be dealt with before your family has to be informed." Mr. Albright rose to his feet. "I am very sorry your visit to us has ended in this way."

She watched him go out the far door without turning back, his perfectly tailored shoulders stiff, his white hair gleaming in the light. He had said nothing about putting up bail to have her released. Perhaps, considering the charge, it was not possible anyway. She would stay here, hungry, aching, and cold to the bone. Christmas was ten days away — they might not bring her to trial before then. And when they did — then what? Oh, please heaven he would tell her father, and he would come and shatter this nightmare!

Officer Flannery came to see Jemima late in the afternoon, as it was already getting dark. She saw him in the same bare interview room where she had been charged, sitting on the same wooden-backed chair.

He looked different without his police hat. He had thick dark hair with a heavy curl in it. He looked tired and cold.

"Are you all right?" He asked her the same question Mr. Albright had, and with something of the same anxiety.

"I cannot tell you anything further," she said more stiffly than she had meant to. It was her only defense against showing the fear and misery she felt. "I did not see Mrs. Cardew alive, except for a few moments in the park the previous afternoon, when she turned toward us and looked up at the snow on the branches. I would not even know it was the same woman if Harley had not told me. But he knew her; I did not."

"Are you certain that you didn't, Miss Pitt?" he said gravely.

"Yes, of course I am. I've only just

arrived in New York." Surely he must know that?

"Actually, you arrived over a week ago," he pointed out. "At exactly the same time as Miss Cardew."

"I know that!" Then she felt the chill of a new apprehension. What did he mean? There was no accusation in his eyes, only sadness.

"Did Miss Cardew know that her mother was in the city?" he asked.

"Of course not!" Jemima protested. "That is what Harley and I were trying to do — stop Maria Cardew from turning up and creating a scene, upsetting Phinnie at the wedding. Didn't he tell you that?"

"He seems to now think that it is possible she *did* know," Flannery replied.

Jemima was astonished. Suddenly nothing made sense. "If she knows it is because *he* told her! But why would he do that?" She was utterly confused. "Harley wanted the whole wedding to be a high-society event, with no hint of scandal to mar it. He told me he was even willing to pay Maria Cardew to stay away."

"That would've been an extraordinarily foolish thing to do. If she was the kind of woman he said, then she could extort him for the rest of her life."

"I told him that!" She could feel fear sharpening her voice, building up inside her like a trapped thing, ready to lash out. "I said there would be no end of it!"

"I want to believe you, Miss Pitt," Flannery said gently, "but the only thing in your favor is that he says it is possible that Miss Cardew not only knew that her mother was in New York, but also knew where she was."

"If that is true then Harley told her," she said again desperately.

"Yes, maybe . . ."

"Are you sure you didn't tell her, even unintentionally?" There was an urgency in his voice, as if the grief of this tragedy touched him too. "Perhaps she would be able to piece it together from other things you said. Could she have guessed? Might she have known what you were doing anyway? If you mentioned where you had been that afternoon, could she have worked it out that her mother was there?" Flannery looked as if he wanted any of those options to be true almost as much as she did.

Jemima steadied herself with an effort. She must keep some control. Just at the moment it was her only chance to save herself.

"Even if she had worked that out from something I said, that doesn't explain how Harley knew that she knew."

"Perhaps he is trying to help you, Miss Pitt. It would be in your interest if she did know. Then at least there is another person to suspect of having killed Maria Cardew." He looked at her steadily, his eyes intensely blue.

"Harley would never accuse Phinnie of such a thing. And Phinnie wouldn't do that," she said miserably. "And I'm not going to try to blame her. She can be selfish and a bit silly at times — she's terribly young — but she wouldn't stab anyone to death, let alone her own mother! She just wouldn't. Apart from anything else, she hasn't the courage or the emotional intensity."

He smiled a little ruefully.

"Honest, if not flattering," he said.

"I don't think I can afford to be anything but honest," she confessed. And then she wondered, for a moment, if perhaps Phinnie wanted the marriage to Brent Albright enough to have elicited the information from Harley, and then crept out to try to persuade her mother herself. Could she have offered to keep her in comfort for the rest of her life, if she just let the marriage take place without upsetting anything? Once married to Brent, Phinnie would have the means. If the marriage did not go ahead, then she wouldn't! If Maria Cardew was as greedy and ruthless as Harley had said, she would understand that.

Was that impossible?

She said all this to Flannery, stumbling over the words, hating the sound of them in her own ears.

He looked unhappy, but he did not argue.

She knew the inevitable ending to her train of thought. She gave it words before he could: "Even if all that was true, Phinnie had no reason to kill Mrs. Cardew. Why would she? She would just pay her off until such time as the Albrights could deal with her more effectively."

"Maybe she didn't want them to know?" he responded. Now he was arguing to defend Jemima!

She shook her head. Phinnie would never manage to keep something like this from Brent.

Officer Flannery pushed his hand through his hair in a gesture of exasperation. "I'm trying to help you!"

"Thank you," she said with a

laugh that turned into a sob. "But are you sure you should be?"

"I don't think you killed her," he replied. "I just don't know who did."

"The door was open. Anyone could have gone in."

"Why would they? Nothing was taken. There wasn't much to take. No one else was seen. We spoke to all the other residents. No one saw anybody else."

"I didn't touch her," Jemima said yet again. "She was dead when I got there."

"Have you had anyone tell your family you're in trouble?" Flannery asked her.

"Mr. Albright said he would, if we couldn't sort it out quickly without their having to know. It would take my father a week or more to get here anyway. And what would he do?" That was a possibility she had not even thought about before, and in spite of her best effort she could feel the tears prickle behind her eyes, and the lump in her throat become almost too large to swallow.

Flannery stood up. He looked stiff and awkward.

"I'll sort it out before then," he promised, the color hot in his cheeks. "You won't need him to come."

Jemima remembered those words all afternoon, sitting alone in her cell with its solitary window far above her eye level. She could hear other women prisoners shouting and sometimes even laughing, but it was a hard, raucous sound, totally without pleasure.

The white light, reflected off the snow, was beginning to fade. She was finding it very hard to keep hope when one of the guards returned, brandishing the keys.

"Your lucky day," he said without a smile. "Someone put up bail for you." He unlocked the door noisily and pulled it wide. "I guess that means we don't have to give you supper."

Mr. Albright? Harley, relenting? It was his testimony that had put her here, at least mostly. Or Phinnie? Maybe she had prevailed upon

Brent to come?

"Thank you," she said to the guard, and went out through the iron-bar door as quickly as she could. "How do I get . . . ?" And then she wondered if she would be welcomed back into the Albright house. Perhaps not. Where could she stay? She couldn't leave the city because she was on bail, but she did not have sufficient money to pay for her own lodgings for as long as it might be before she came to trial. It was midwinter, nearly Christmas. She would freeze to death without shelter. The streets would be worse than jail.

The guard was looking at her. He sighed. "She's out there waiting for you. You'd better get out of here before she changes her mind."

Jemima's heart rose. It must be Phinnie after all. Phinnie, of all people, had realized that she could never have hurt Maria Cardew, let alone killed her.

"Thank you," she said hastily to the guard. Then she followed him along the stone passageway and, this time, out as far as the entrance.

But it was not Phinnie who stood waiting for her; it was Celia Albright. She was wearing a very ordinary dark cape over her dress and a hat that could have belonged to anyone. She seemed to have shrunken into herself, her shoulders hunched wearily. However, her face lit up with relief when she saw Jemima and she moved toward her quickly, searching her face.

"Are you all right? No one has hurt you?"

"I am perfectly well," Jemima answered as levelly as she could, but her voice was thick with emotion. "Just cold and . . . frightened."

"Of course you are," Celia agreed. "Come, we must get out of here as quickly as possible. It is a dreadful place. The carriage is waiting around the corner; there is no room for it here." She led the way at a brisk pace and, all but treading on her heels, Jemima followed. It was getting dark and the street-lights, less elegant in this part of the city, were beginning to glow brightly.

As soon as they were seated in the

carriage, it moved away.

"Thank you," Jemima said again, meaning it with a depth of feeling she could not conceal.

Celia's face was unreadable in the shadows, but her voice was tense.

"I would be grateful if you did not mention it to Mr. Albright — in fact, to anyone in the family. It could lead to . . . unpleasantness."

Jemima was puzzled. "Did Mr. Albright not —"

"No," Celia cut her off. "I did it myself, with Farrell's help. Rothwell may guess that, but I would prefer that he did not know it. I doubt he will ask me."

Jemima was stunned. The family had been prepared to leave her in jail, perhaps even over Christmas!

Fight for her, pay a lawyer, perhaps, but only because she was connected to them as Phinnie's friend.

"Did Phinnie ask you to?" she said impulsively.

Celia remained staring ahead. "No," she replied very quietly. Jemima had to strain to hear the words. "Please do not ask me any further questions, Miss Pitt. I prefer not to answer you. I do not know what happened to Mrs. Cardew, but I don't believe that you had anything to do with it, except unintentionally. But not everyone agrees with me."

Jemima took several moments to weigh what she had heard. Why would anyone imagine she could have so savagely killed Maria

Cardew, a woman she had never met and who had nothing to do with her life? Could they really believe that Phinnie had asked her to do it and she had agreed? Whatever kind of person did they think Phinnie was? She was in love with Brent, certainly. Her only dream was to be his wife. Yes, she liked the wealth and the position in society, but the idea that she would kill for those things was absurd.

The murderer must have been someone from Maria's past life, whatever she had been doing over the years between leaving Mr. Cardew and finding herself in the cheapest of lodging houses in New York. It was just the most wretched of misfortunes that Harley and

Jemima had found her on the day of her death. Such coincidences were rare, but of course they did happen.

What was it going to be like living in the Albright mansion from now until Christmas, and then the wedding, under the shadow of suspicion? She could hardly attend parties with people wondering if she had knifed a woman to death!

But would they know? What had the newspapers said? She needed to be aware of that before she arrived. She turned to Celia again.

"Miss Albright . . ."

"Yes?"

"What have the newspapers said? Did they name me?"

"No. Rothwell managed to prevent that. And of course Mrs. Cardew was not named either. And he simply told Phinnie the barest of facts, which was both a sadness to her and something of a relief. She no longer has to fear that her mother might turn up at the wedding, or one of the parties, and cause the most acute embarrassment."

Jemima tried to imagine it. "It would have been unfortunate," she agreed. "But not so terrible . . ."

"Phinnie has been told that Maria drank," Celia explained. "So far as I know, that is not true. She has also been told that her mother was of extremely loose morals with regard to men. That is . . . questionable. I would have said she had somewhat eccentric tastes, which is not at all the same as being loose."

Any further conversation was prevented by their arrival at the Albright mansion. It was completely dark. They were only a moment or two on the lighted front step, and then in the warmth of the bright hall. The butler greeted Celia with respect and Jemima with civility.

"I am sure you would like something hot to eat," Celia said as they crossed the hall under the blazing chandelier. "The family is dining out. I am not hungry, but you may have your food brought up to your room; or, if you prefer, you can eat in the kitchen. I do that myself occasionally, and it is very pleasant, and rather more comfortable than dining in a bedroom. I do not care for the odor of food remaining all night."

"Thank you," Jemima said, accepting. "The kitchen sounds a good idea, and will be less troublesome to the staff. You don't think they will mind my presence?"

For the first time, Celia smiled with genuine warmth. "You have been most courteous to them, my dear. They will not mind in the least." There was a wealth of implication hidden in her words, but Jemima did not pursue it, although the ideas whirled in her mind later as she sat at a bench in the kitchen and enjoyed one of the best meals she had eaten since leaving home. She could hear Lucy, the chambermaid, giggling in the pantry and every now and then the footman's voice singing a snatch from one of the latest musical shows — "Give my regards to Broadway, remember me to Herald Square . . ."

Cook was rolling her eyes and muttering, but nothing unkind. Violet, the scullery maid, was sweeping the floor, the broom making a swishing sound over the stones. Billy, the boot boy, was re-stoking the stove. It was warm and familiar in the way that well-used kitchens are.

The following morning at the breakfast table it was very different. Jemima arrived at the usual time that the meal was served. The last thing she wanted was to cause inconvenience by being either early or late. Everyone else was present. They all looked up as she came into the room and took the same chair as she had previously, the only one currently unoccupied.

"Good morning," she said quietly.

Mr. Albright looked up from his plate and replied politely but without expression.

"Good morning, Miss Pitt," Brent answered. He looked at her guardedly, his light eyes distant, as though she were the merest acquaintance. Perhaps he was withholding judgment, but certainly he had not acquitted her in his mind.

Harley glanced at her without speaking at all, and continued with his meal.

Phinnie was very smartly dressed in clothes Jemima knew she had not brought with her. They were the height of fashion, big-sleeved and wide-skirted, actually rather too old for her, dominating her youthful beauty.

"Good morning, Jemima," Phinnie said coolly, then searched for something else to say, and found nothing.

Only Celia addressed Jemima with warmth. "Good morning, Miss Pitt. I hope you slept well?"

Harley glared at her but she ignored him, continuing to speak to Jemima.

"I am going shopping in the middle of the day, and will take luncheon in town. Perhaps you would like to accompany me?"

"Is that wise, Aunt Celia?" Brent asked, frowning at her.

Celia's temper was raw and she clearly held it in with difficulty. "What are you suggesting, Brent? That we require Miss Pitt to spend the rest of her time as our guest sitting in her room? It is still nine days until Christmas, and two weeks until the wedding."

"I am aware what day it is," Brent replied. "It is the middle of winter and everything is covered with snow. It is not a great hardship to stay in a well-heated house with a library and a music room, and servants to bring you anything you might wish. Most people would count themselves very fortunate to enjoy such a life."

Phinnie looked at him, her eyes soft and bright, then back at Celia. "Brent is right. I'm sure Jemima will be very comfortable, and grateful for your hospitality." Her voice quivered a little on the last sentence, but it was impossible to tell what emotion moved her. It could have been pity, fear of the future, an ever-increasing devotion to Brent, or anxiety that he thought Jemima guilty of some kind of complicity in Maria's death. It might even have been grief. Even so, Jemima did not care for being spoken around, as if she were not present to answer for herself.

Harley looked at them one by

one, and said nothing. He seemed to be watching, waiting for something.

Jemima looked at Celia. "Thank you," she said sincerely. "I would be delighted to come with you. To walk a little would be very pleasant, and I should enjoy your company."

Jemima was in the hall, with her overcoat on, waiting for Celia, when Phinnie came over to her. Her brows were drawn down and her expression was one of annoyance.

"Jemima, are you deliberately trying to spoil my wedding?" She said it quietly, so no nearby servant could overhear her, but with an edge of real anger in her tone. "Celia was just being pleasant to you! Can't you see that? The last thing she wants is to be seen with you in public. Mr. Albright paid to have you released because he is a good man. That doesn't mean anyone here thinks you are innocent!"

Jemima felt as if she had been slapped. No wonder Celia did not wish the rest of the family to know that it was she who had paid Jemima's bail, presumably with her own money!

"Indeed?" Jemima said coldly. "And does that include you?"

"What can I think?" Phinnie demanded. "That it was some lunatic off the street? Why? From what Harley said, she had nothing to steal. She was found in her own bed, stabbed to death."

"I know that!" Jemima snapped. "I was the one who found her, poor woman."

"She wasn't a 'poor woman,' " Phinnie said bitterly. "She had everything — a good and decent husband, kind, respected, and wealthy — and she left him . . . and me . . . to go back to a life on the streets. No one forced her to do that, she was just a . . . a whore! She chose that, no one made her. Some women have no choice; she had every choice in the world." Now tears were running down her face and her voice was all but choked.

Jemima felt the burning pain and

injustice of the situation, and a terrible pity for Phinnie. Her own childhood was filled with memories of love, laughter, and adventures, long, lovely days spent mostly with her mother and her brother, Daniel, as well. Phinnie had had none of that.

But no matter what Maria Cardew had been, or what she had done that was selfish, or even lewd or revolting, it didn't change the fact that Jemima had not hurt her.

"I did not kill her, Phinnie," she said firmly. "I have no idea who did. I just found her."

"Why?" Phinnie challenged. "Why were you even looking for her?"

"Because Harley asked me to help

him."

Phinnie's eyebrows rose. "Why would Harley want to find her?"

"For heaven's sake!" Jemima said desperately. "To make sure she didn't interrupt your wedding and embarrass you! Or embarrass the family, of course," she added, remembering that Phinnie must know Harley as well as she did.

The color bleached out of Phinnie's face and she looked stunned. "Harley asked *you*? That's not what he said . . ."

"Really?" Jemima should not have been surprised. Except the thought that came fleetingly to her mind was whether it was Harley who was lying or Phinnie. "Think about it," she went on. "How would I even know that your mother was in New York, let alone where to look for her?"

"Then . . . then maybe it was Celia," Phinnie suggested. "She's known my mother for years. She pretends to have liked her, but she's very protective of the family. She would be; it's her family too."

"You aren't suggesting that Celia killed your mother, surely?" Jemima was aghast. It was a monstrous notion. "Why, for heaven's sake? That makes no sense at all!" And the moment the words were out of her mouth, she knew that it made very ugly sense, even though she could not believe it.

Phinnie met her eyes boldly. "Yes, it does. When I marry Brent, I will be mistress of this house. What will she be? I could understand it if she were not willing to see that happen."

Jemima looked at her icily. "Yes, I believe you could. You have the advantage of me. I hadn't even considered such a thing."

Phinnie's face tightened. She recognized the insult. "There's rather a lot you don't consider," she retaliated. "You'll probably end up like Celia, being hostess and housekeeper for your brother, if he marries and then loses his wife. Although of course he won't have the Albright power or influence. Hardly anybody else has."

"You really value that, don't you?" Jemima stared at Phinnie as if she had not truly seen her before. "How far would you go to make sure you get it? The police thought you might have done it yourself, you know? I told them that was impossible. That you were not the kind of person who would even think of such a thing. Perhaps I was wrong?"

Phinnie blushed scarlet. "You told them that?"

"Yes. And you're right, I am naïve," Jemima replied. "But perhaps they will discover that for themselves." She turned to walk away, but Phinnie grasped her arm and held her back.

"Jemima!" She gulped. "I'm sorry. I didn't mean it. I'm horribly confused. I hated my mother all my life, because she left me and my father. I know it hurt him too. He never even imagined loving anyone else. But now that she's dead, and in such an awful way, I'm sad that I'll never know her. I didn't think I wanted to, but I'm not sure." She gulped. "Above all, I love Brent so much it makes me sick to think that anything could go wrong with our wedding. I know what I said about the Albright name, but it really doesn't matter to me. In fact, at times I wish we were quite ordinary, then there wouldn't be all this pressure to do everything the right way all the time. It's like . . . like being royalty. I don't really want to be a princess. I just want to be with Brent."

Jemima smiled in spite of her own confusion of emotions. Did she believe Phinnie? Yes, at least in part. Everything she had said was true. But there was a lingering presence there of passion to succeed, at any cost. She had been so quick to blame Jemima. The kind of love she felt was like a fever. It overcame everything else and destroyed the restraints she might normally have exercised.

"Jemima!" Phinnie said urgently. "You must believe me!"

"Of course," Jemima agreed quietly, and it was almost true. Phinnie wouldn't let Jemima go to trial for a murder she had not committed — well, probably she wouldn't. Before Phinnie could see the doubt in her eyes, she turned and walked away. Phinnie called after her, but she pretended not to have heard. She was surprised by how hurt she felt, and by how frightened she was.

That night Jemima did not sleep well. She woke up often and, even though the room was well heated, she felt cold and stiff. There was no sound, not even that of the wind outside the window. She opened the curtains and saw everything cloaked with snow, the huge city lit as if it too were awake, but frozen into lifelessness. She had been here less than two weeks, but she had learned to like New York — the vitality, the strange mixture of peoples.

And yet she was terribly alone, and accused of a crime for which her life could be taken. And there was no one to help her but herself.

If she was her father's daughter, that should be enough. Thomas Pitt had been a regular policeman, solving murders just like this one, before he joined Special Branch.

She went back to bed and lay with the covers up to her chin, trying to get warm again, and concentrated her thoughts. What would he advise her to do? Certainly not give up and wait for help, or lie here feeling sorry for herself and hope that the police went on looking for the answer. Why should they not accept that the foreign young woman who had found the body was not as guilty as she seemed?

Patrick Flannery's strong face with its gentleness and humor came into her mind, and she forced herself to dismiss it.

Her only defense was to attack. In the morning she would get up early, have breakfast in the kitchen, and then go out and begin to look for the truth. Nothing had been stolen, Phinnie had said, and a glance at Maria's possessions and style of life would have been enough to know there was nothing worth taking. The knife, the violence of the wound that had killed her, made it clear that bringing about her death was the sole purpose of her assailant. So it was someone who knew her.

Then Jemima must learn to know her also. How long had Maria lived there? Who were her friends, and her enemies? Who might believe she had wronged them, or was a threat to them? And why? What could she know of anyone that was worth such a violent and terrible way of preventing her from telling it?

By nine o'clock the next morning, Jemima was already at the apartment building where Maria Cardew had lived, blinking against the flat, white light reflected off the snow. She had chosen different clothes from the ones she'd had on when she was here with Harley, and she'd pinned her hair up in as different a style as it would take.

She had planned what to say. She was less than satisfied with it, but all the alternatives she could think of were even worse. It was always best to stick as close to the truth as possible. It was easier to remember, and one was less likely to make an irretrievable error. Apart from that, consistently lying took up a great deal of one's emotional energy, and that in itself often gave one away.

"Good morning," she said cheerfully to the first woman she met as she stood in the hallway. Of course the one thing she could not disguise was her English accent. Her voice would betray her every time.

"Mornin'," the woman replied, at first barely glancing at Jemima, then stopping and looking at her again more carefully.

Now was the time for the first invention. It might be passed around within hours, so she must be careful what she said. "I wonder if you can help me." She smiled tentatively. "The woman who died up on the third floor —"

The face of the woman in front of her hardened. "If you're from one o' those newspapers, you can just turn around and go right back where you came from!" she said tartly. "She were a good-livin' woman, an' I got nothin' to say." She started to move away.

"I'm not!" Jemima said sharply, taking a step after her. "She has English family. I want to be able to write to them and tell them that she was properly cared for, and there were people to speak well of her . . ."

The woman stopped and looked back. She surveyed Jemima up and down, and Jemima met her eyes with total innocence. So far what she had said was the truth.

"So what do you want to know, then?" the woman said cautiously. "She's gone, poor soul. Can't do nothin' for her now."

"I can speak well of her reputation," Jemima replied. "I think I would want that after my death, wouldn't you?"

"I s'pose," the woman conceded. "She deserved it, anyhow."

Jemima smiled. "It's a horribly

cold morning. Would you like a cup of coffee? There's a place about two blocks away from here. I would be pleased if you would join me."

"There's a better one back there." The woman jerked her head, indicating the opposite direction.

"Excellent," Jemima said immediately. "Please lead the way."

"Don't look nothing from the outside," the woman warned.

"That hardly matters," Jemima replied. "Is it warm?"

The woman smiled. "You bet! My name's Ellie Shultz."

"Jemima Pitt. How do you do?" She held out her hand.

The woman looked puzzled.

"I'm English. That's the way we say hello."

The woman gave a little laugh and took Jemima's hand.

They spoke little on the journey over the freezing pavements. Ellie nodded to several people and called out greetings to others. She was right about the coffee shop. It was shabby, parts of the roof hung with icicles where the gutters had broken, but inside was warm and several people welcomed her. The black woman behind the counter gave them a brilliant smile and offered them coffee. At a corner table a man with a thick beard was speaking in Russian to his companion, and laughing jovially at her response.

Ellie gave Jemima a questioning glance, and Jemima smiled her approval. She found it exciting rather than strange, like several districts of London squashed into one.

The coffee smelled every bit as good as Ellie had said, and while it cooled Jemima asked about Maria Cardew.

"That place wasn't really hers," Ellie explained. "It was Sara Godwin's, but she was so sick, poor soul, she couldn't manage. Maria came to see her, and just stayed. Looked after her, she did. Couldn't have been better to her if they'd been sisters. Sat up with her all night sometimes, when she was really bad."

"Oh!" Jemima was surprised by this, but then remembered the empty bed in the flat. "So what happened to Sara Godwin?"

"She got a bit better," Ellie said cheerfully. She blew on her coffee, impatient to be able to drink it. "Last time I saw her she were up and walking. Maria cooked for her an' everything. Kept the place clean, washed the sheets and that sort of thing. Poor Sara was too sick to do it herself. Not that she wouldn't have. Just couldn't hardly move."

"But she got better?"

"Yeah. Don't know if it was for keeps, poor thing. But cared for each other, those two. Sara's husband was gone. Died hard, she told me once."

She went on to tell stories of both women. The more Jemima heard, the deeper her sense of loss became. She could not help seeing Maria Cardew's face as she had looked up at the snow on the trees in Central Park, and the joy that had been in it.

"But where did Sara Godwin go?" she asked at length, when they had finished their third cup of the best coffee she had ever tasted.

Ellie shook her head. "I dunno. Some man was looking for her, last I heard. Didn't mean her any good, I'd bet. She must have gone to get away from him. Maybe she'll be back. She didn't take much with her."

"Did Maria tell you that?"

"She said somebody'd followed Sara. Wish I knew she were all right. Course, she'll be torn up to pieces about Maria." She sniffed. "A good few people will be." She looked hard at Jemima. "You see they speak right about her! I don't know who did that to her, and likely they'll never find out. Far as the police think, she was just another woman nobody wanted. But you can't help it if you lose your folks and there's no one to care. Woman on your own doesn't mean you're a whore!"

Jemima had a sudden vision of loneliness, poverty, always dealing with judgments based on ignorance and fighting for warmth and a place to belong. Why on earth had Maria Cardew left all the safety of an excellent marriage in England,

and her own small child who desperately needed her, for such a life?

"Thank you," she said with a wave of feeling. "If she was kind to someone in need, that repays a multitude of past errors . . . if there were any."

"You'll say something good of her?"

"I will."

After leaving the coffee shop Jemima started to walk around the neighborhood, looking for the places where Maria might have shopped, eaten — specifically, bought food, or medicines for her friend Sara Godwin.

She moved slowly along the busy streets. In this poorer area they were far narrower than the avenues where the Albrights lived, but there was a variety in them that fascinated her. Strange foods were displayed like works of art — lots of pickles, cuts of meat she had never seen before, and every kind of sausage you could imagine, some with rich-colored skins. She knew enough to recognize some Italian names, and some German. Others she couldn't even attempt to pronounce.

She saw women with different clothes, concealing their hair, and wondered if they would look half so mysterious dressed like anyone else. Their manner of dress concentrated attention on their marvelous eyes, full of expression. She wondered what their thoughts were of her. With her fair skin and auburn-tinted hair, she probably looked Irish to them!

After some questions, and a little laughter at her accent, she found an apothecary shop that seemed to stock a rich variety of medicines, all known by their Latin names.

She was trying to describe Maria Cardew to the woman at the counter when she heard an Irish voice behind her. She swiveled around and saw Officer Patrick Flannery standing about a yard away. He was not surprised to see her, although he would hardly have recognized her from the back. He must have heard her voice.

"Are you ill?" he asked with some concern.

"No, not at all . . ." Then she realized that she had little option but to tell him the truth. It was going to come out anyway, as soon as he spoke to the woman behind the counter. She must remember what her father had said about lies revealing more about you than the truth would.

"I met a woman who knew Maria Cardew. I wanted to hear about her, so I asked. The woman said Maria looked after a sick friend, Sara Godwin. I thought Maria might have bought her medicines here."

"What difference would that make?"

"It would be a record of Maria Cardew looking after someone with considerable kindness. It would show she wasn't the kind of person Harley Albright said she was." Why did she have to explain that to him? Surely it was easy enough to understand. And why was she disappointed that he was so slow? She would probably never see him again, unless he came to arrest her!

"Does that matter to you, Miss Pitt?" His voice was still gentle.

"Yes." She thought of the face of the woman in the park. "Yes, it does. I saw her alive only once, but there was something good in her. I don't believe Phinnie hurt her mother, and I want her to have at least one pleasant memory of Maria. You can't discard parents, even if you want to. They are part of who you are."

For a moment there was raw emotion in Flannery's face also, a mixture of pity and joy. "No, surely you can't!" he agreed. "And it'd be the last thing I'd want. My mother is the best woman I've ever known." Then, as if embarrassed by his feelings, he went on quickly, "But I doubt you'd persuade Miss Delphinia Cardew of that. She hasn't a nice thing to say about her mother."

"Don't take her too seriously," Jemima pleaded. "She's never known why Maria left her as a tiny child. It seems nobody knows. And now, when perhaps she could have met her and made some reconciliation, Maria is dead, and we'll never understand."

"She might have killed Maria herself, and yet you're out here in the snow, walking around the back streets trying to find out something positive to tell her?" he asked in amazement.

Now it was Jemima who felt embarrassed. "I have other reasons. Don't you think I killed Maria? Nobody seems to be doing anything to prove otherwise. I need to defend myself, and the only way I can do that is by finding out who really did kill her."

"So you're beginning by looking for every fine thing she did, any kindness, maybe every lame dog she helped over a stile?" he asked with a trace of humor.

"I'm trying to find out anything I

can about her!" she said sharply. "She was stabbed to death with a knife, probably from her own kitchen — or actually Sara Godwin's kitchen. Somebody must've hated her pretty badly. That's who I'm looking for. I haven't done very well so far, but then, I started only this morning."

It sounded ridiculous, put like that, and not only stupid but also hopeless. Suddenly she felt small and cold and very silly. She should never have left London, where she was safe and had her family to believe in her and help her.

She swallowed the lump in her throat and stared back at Officer Flannery. "Someone killed her, and whatever you think, I know it was not I!"

He looked at her as if she were a lost child. "I think here's a smart place to start," he said. He looked past her to the woman behind the counter. "What did you sell to Mrs. Cardew, please, ma'am? We need to find as many people she knew as we can, so we can learn a thing or two about her. Then we'll leave your shop, so you can be getting on with your business." He smiled at her, looking kind, but also large and stubborn and very official.

The woman pulled out her records and told him everything she knew. Maria Cardew had spent quite a lot of money on medicine for Sara.

"And did she happen to mention

her friend's illness?" Flannery asked.

"Consumption," the woman answered. "The poor soul. No cure for that, but Mrs. Cardew made her life a lot easier. Had some real strong spells, she did."

"Thank you." Patrick Flannery smiled at her and the woman looked pleased.

Outside on the pavement he stopped, standing closer to the street than Jemima, protecting her from the splashes of passing vehicles.

"And what did you plan to do next?" he asked.

"Food shops," she answered. "She might have bought special items for Sara. There might even be a doctor . . ."

"Are you sure you want to do this?" he said doubtfully. "You might find she wasn't as nice as you think."

"Of course," Jemima said quickly. "I don't believe she was a saint. If she was, then why did someone kill her?"

"Well, I suppose there's the chance she knew something that was dangerous," he said. "She might unintentionally have witnessed an argument or a fight, someone making an illegal deal or . . ." He stopped abruptly, a faint color in his cheeks.

She laughed, then instantly wished she had not. It would have been far more ladylike to have affected not to know what he meant. "I'm sorry," she said contritely.

He blinked and shook his head. "Don't apologize. Perhaps I shouldn't have said —"

"Of course you should. She may very easily have seen somebody where they should not have been, or with someone they should not have been with. But how do we find out what, if anything, she knew? And if it really mattered so much as to kill her for it."

"High society is very proper in New York," he told her quickly.

Jemima was taken aback. Did he consider her part of that high society and somehow worry that he had offended her by being so candid? How could she undo that impression?

"I know that," she said. "I am staying with the Albrights, remember? They are far more correct than anyone I know at home. But . . ."

"But what?" he asked, now watching her very carefully, although she did not know what the intensity in his face meant. She was beginning to feel self-conscious.

"But very often, the higher up in society you get, the less 'proper' you are," she answered. "My great-grandaunt Lady Narraway's father was an earl, and she is the most outrageous person I know. I think you would like her enormously, though that is a little presumptuous of me to say."

"Do you like her?" he asked with

interest.

"As much as anyone I've ever known," she answered without hesitation. "When she was young she was said to be the most beautiful woman in Europe. Now she is far older, and I think she still is. But she is brave and funny and terribly wise, which is what matters."

"In what way is she wise?" He was asking because he wanted to know. There was no challenge in his voice, or in the expression in his eyes.

She thought for a moment. She wanted him to understand what she meant. It mattered to her, but she wanted to do Aunt Vespasia justice as well, and that was not easy.

"She knows what matters and what doesn't," she answered, choosing her words carefully. "She remembers what she receives, but never what she gives. She doesn't hold grudges, and if she thinks something is funny she will laugh, whether it is the 'done thing' or not. She loves the opera, and gorgeous clothes. She is honest when it is fashionable not to be, but she is never unnecessarily unkind. And she will fight to the death for a cause she believes in."

"Do you wish to be like her?" he said gravely.

She did not have to consider that. "Yes," she said instantly. "Yes, I would like that more than anything else."

His expression was hard to read, as if powerful emotions were in conflict inside him.

"Then please take care of yourself," he said softly, "so that you may have the opportunity to do that. You've given me many ideas about where to look for Maria Cardew's killer. You need to be careful. Whoever it is won't want to be found."

"Of course not," Jemima agreed. "And I am not at all sure that the Albrights wish the matter given any more coverage in the news than has already been given."

"Well, you are not going to wander around the streets in a neighborhood like this, asking questions about a murdered woman," he said sternly. "That is the perfect way to get hurt."

"I'll be careful," she promised.

"No, you won't. You'll follow any clues you find and walk all around here, up back alleys and into places where you won't be welcome," he argued. "I can't let you do that."

"But you can let me be convicted of something horrible that I didn't do?"

His face looked pinched. She had hurt him.

"I'm not going to let that happen either," he said rashly. "I'm coming with you. I'll find whoever really killed her, and you'll be safe."

For a moment she saw in his eyes something beautiful, and then she looked away. She could not afford such thoughts. The New York police believed she had stuck a knife into the heart of Maria Cardew. If she were to survive, she must prove that she had not, and the only way to do that was to discover who had.

"Thank you," she acknowledged. "Where shall we begin?"

He made a sharp little sound that she thought was laughter.

"Continue," he corrected. "As you see very logically, it was a crime of deep emotion. Someone either hated her or was frightened of her. The only reason for fear of an elderly woman in her state of health must have been that she had knowledge that could have ruined someone."

"We don't know that she was ill;

that was her friend Sara Godwin," Jemima pointed out. "Why can't we find her? Wouldn't she know who might have killed Maria?"

"We can look for her, but she might be anywhere. She could even be dead, given that she was so ill. She must have had a hard life. She probably worked too much and didn't eat very well." There was pity in his voice, and Jemima liked him for that. It made her think for a moment of her father. He was always sympathizing with the wrong people — at least, wrong as far as both the police and society were concerned.

Then she forced that thought out of her mind. If she were to think of home and family at the moment, she would dissolve in tears and that would be both embarrassing and useless.

They were sheltered where they stood, but it was time to move. For a start, walking would get the blood circulating again, and make them warm, even if it took them away from the narrow alley and into the broader, straighter streets, where the buildings on either side funneled the east wind off the water.

"Where are we going?" she asked after several minutes.

"Best local bakery," he answered. "Then the butcher. She'll have made chicken soup, maybe got bits and pieces many folk don't want. My mother used to do that, when times were harder."

Jemima kept up with Flannery's pace with difficulty. He had not stopped to think that while she was tall for a woman, she was still several inches shorter than he, and wearing heeled boots and a heavy skirt. It was a kind of oblique compliment that she did not want to spoil by lagging behind.

She tried to think what kind of information Maria Cardew could have had that could be so dangerous. At her age it didn't seem likely that she was having inappropriate relations with anyone. And anyone important enough to matter would not be frequenting this area. The locals around here were immigrants, the hardworking poor.

They reached the poultry shop,

and yes, the owner knew Maria quite well, kept good pieces for her and slipped them in with the other bits he sold her cheaply. He was distressed to hear of her death.

"She was a good woman," he said, pulling his mouth into an expression of disgust at such a tragedy. "Always had a pleasant word. I don't know what the world's coming to." He glared at Flannery. "And what are you doing about it, eh? Just one poor old woman, no money, no power, so what does it matter?" He sighed, shaking his head.

"We're going to find out who did it," Jemima said firmly. "But it isn't easy. For a start, why would anyone do that? She had nothing worth taking."

The butcher stared at her. "Who are you? You talk oddly."

"I'm English," she explained. "I know some of her family, and I liked her. I want to know what happened."

"She wasn't English. She was as American as anyone. She was born here!" He made it a challenge.

"I know. But she lived in England for a while. She was married to an Englishman."

"Oh?" He raised his eyebrows. "She didn't say anything about that. Only man I ever saw her with was black!"

There was a moment of silence, then Flannery spoke.

"Black? Did you know him?"

The man shook his head. "Not from round here. But he spoke regular, so he could have been from anywhere. He didn't mean her harm. Spoke softly to her, and she to him."

"But she knew him?" Flannery said.

"Only saw him a couple of times. Like I said, not from round here."

Flannery leaned forward a little. "Help me to find who killed her, sir. I need to know about her for that. It wasn't any passing robbery. Whoever did it did it violently, and there was hatred in it."

The man winced. "You could try Dr. Vine, down the road a couple of blocks, number 416. His real name is something longer, Russian

or Polish, that sort of thing. Everyone calls him Dr. Vine. She went to
him for her friend."

"Thank you." Flannery accepted
the advice and took Jemima by the
arm, guiding her out into the windy
street.

Dr. Vine was as much help as he
could be. He too was distressed to
hear of Maria Cardew's death.

"Can't tell you much, except that
Sara Godwin could not have managed without Maria's care." He
shook his head. "Great shame.
Don't know how the poor soul will
get on now. Have you seen her?"

"No," Flannery said quickly. "We
thought she'd gone before Mrs.
Cardew was killed." Now he looked
anxious. "There was no sign of her

in the apartment, and she doesn't appear to have returned since. I've been keeping an eye on the place."

"Could be she died anyway, before Maria was killed," Dr. Vine said unhappily.

"I'll check the city records," Flannery promised. "If she died, somebody will know. Thank you, Dr. Vine."

But no city records of recent deaths showed any sign of Sara Godwin. The following day, Jemima and Officer Flannery looked at the residential records. The clerk stood beside the bench with the ledger in his arms.

"I don't know what you're trying to find," he said as if he were afraid of being overheard. "But you should be careful, sir." He spoke only to Flannery. "I suppose you already know it, but the woman who was murdered in that building was related to Miss Delphinia Cardew, her that's getting married to Mr. Brent Albright."

"Yes, I know," Flannery answered. "Nobody seems to know much about her."

"No, sir, I suppose they don't. But we know a lot about the Albright family, and most of us know enough not to upset them by asking a whole lot of personal questions. Do a very great deal for this city, they do. And doesn't do to fall out with people with that kind of power, if you get my meaning?"

Jemima started to speak, but

Flannery put his hand on her arm, closing his grasp firmly enough for her to fall silent.

"Better to clear this up now, rather than later, don't you think?" he said politely to the clerk. "I'm sure Mr. Albright would like to have the matter settled, and then not raised again. Over with, if you see what I mean?"

"Ah!" The clerk nodded and a smile spread slowly across his face. He touched one finger to the side of his nose in a gesture of understanding. "Then I'll just leave these with you, sir." He looked at Jemima. "Ma'am."

Jemima realized with horror that the clerk thought Flannery was here to serve the Albright family, not Maria Cardew. He had assumed that even the police were bought, one way or another.

"Don't look like that!" Flannery let go of her arm. "Your face gives you away!"

She could not think of anything to say. He had read her thoughts perfectly, and it was at once frightening and comforting. She wanted him to understand her. It was the end of a kind of loneliness, and yet it was the beginning of a new experience that could be too enormous to handle.

She swallowed. "Are the Albrights really so important?"

"Yes. Didn't you know that?" He put his hand back on her arm, but this time lightly. She could see his fingers on her coat sleeve rather than feel them. "Albright and Cardew make millions of dollars. All the power rests in the two families. When the present generation dies, or retires, it will all pass to Mr. Albright's sons."

"And Phinnie," Jemima added. "I wonder why Maria Cardew came back to New York. Was it really to try to see her daughter? She must have known the Albrights would not want her here. Was she hiding so close to them with the hope that they would never look for her on their own doorstep?"

Patrick was looking through the ledger as he spoke. "Could be. America is a huge country, thousands of miles across. She could have gone West and disappeared if she had truly wanted to." He went on leafing through the pages.

"Then she had a reason to be here," Jemima concluded. "It must have been a very strong one, Officer Flannery . . ."

He looked up. "You are not under arrest, Jemima. Do you think you could call me Patrick?"

She felt the color burn up her face, but she liked the idea. In fact, it had been in her mind when she thought of him, and she had had to remind herself not to use it.

"Patrick," she began again, a little self-consciously. "She must have had a very important reason for coming back here."

"Perhaps she knew that Harley

Albright would pay her well to stay away from the wedding."

"Then who killed her? Did he?" she asked him. It seemed far-fetched, but it wasn't impossible.

"Or Delphinia herself," he replied. "I know you hate the thought, but she's a healthy young woman. It wouldn't be out of the question for her to have driven that knife through her mother's chest, especially since she would be the last one Maria would suspect. Face it, Jemima, she had the best motive of all. She's in love with Brent. She might have convinced herself she was protecting him."

"If she were really protecting him, she would have told him about Maria and let him make his own decision," she said hotly. "Or had a smaller wedding privately somewhere where Maria wouldn't have known about it! I think she's in love with being in love!"

"Most of us would like to be in love," he said very gently. "Wouldn't you, one day?"

She did not dare meet his eyes in case she gave herself away. "Oh, I expect so," she said as lightly as she could. "But I hope it would never bring me to a point where I could consider doing something so . . ."

"Crazy?" he suggested. "Probably not. But love can be pretty overwhelming. It can make you take risks you wouldn't normally even think of." Then he looked a little uncomfortable, as if he had said more than he meant to. He turned away from her, facing along the street into the wind and snow.

For a wild moment Jemima wondered if the reason he was so determined to find Maria's killer and save her from suspicion was that he cared for her. Then she dismissed it as a daydream she couldn't afford to indulge. If they didn't find the real killer, then the police were left with her. She was the one who had found Maria's body, and she had been alone.

"Do you think it could've been the other way around? Brent killed her, out of love for Phinnie?" she asked as sensibly as she could.

"That is possible," he answered slowly, still facing down the street.

"We need to know more about Maria. Her murder might be something to do with her own life, something we missed entirely. Maybe it is only chance that it happened now, so close to the wedding. Come on." He took her arm and started to walk along the pavement briskly, as if he had a specific destination in mind.

Jemima spent the rest of the day with Patrick. They learned more about Maria Cardew, but it was incidental to their search for Sara Godwin. They met many people who knew Sara and spoke well of her. It seemed she was quiet and kept to herself, but was willing to help anyone. But her illness had steadily been getting worse. No one had seen her for several weeks, and frankly, they assumed she had died.

Jemima and Patrick arranged to meet next the morning at the coffee shop to which Ellie Shultz had taken Jemima the previous day. Then Jemima went back to the Albright house feeling both tired and disappointed. She had not said so to Patrick — she had learned rather too quickly to be comfortable using his name — but she was very much aware that they had little time before she would be arrested again, and tried for murder. Only the closeness of Christmas had allowed her even this reprieve.

She hated going back to the Albright mansion, but she had nowhere else to stay. She certainly had not sufficient funds to find herself a room at a hotel of even modest comfort or safety. Added to which her bail was conditional upon her staying where the police could find her at any time.

She had taken off her heavy outdoor coat and was walking across the hall when one of the maids told her that Miss Celia would like to speak with her.

"Thank you," Jemima said with a sinking heart. She had intended to speak with Celia anyway. She owed it to her to keep her apprised of what she had learned, little as it may be. When she went over it in her mind, the information she and Patrick had gathered amounted to nothing that would help. Rather the opposite! Maria Cardew seemed to have been a good woman who was well liked, even respected. Only the Albright family, and Phinnie, had any reason to fear her. And now it looked as if Sara Godwin, the only person who might've been able to shed some light on the matter, was also dead.

She went upstairs to her bedroom, washed, put on dry boots, and then presented herself at Celia's sitting-room door.

The room was warm, both literally from the fire in the hearth and figuratively from the rich colors, the sheen on the polished wood of the furniture, and the wealth of books on the shelves. At any other time, Jemima would have taken great pleasure in being there.

Celia was sitting in one of the armchairs. A piece of embroidery, half finished, lay on top of a sewing basket next to her.

Celia smiled and gestured for her to sit. Jemima accepted gratefully, glad of the warmth, and also very happy to be still at last.

"How are you, Miss Pitt?" Celia said with apparent concern. "I hear from Farrell that you have been out all day. Is that so? The weather is bitter."

Jemima wanted to scream at the banality of the question, but she forced herself to keep calm and respond courteously. "Very well, thank you. I have been outside, but

I am fine."

"Cold, tired, no doubt." Celia smiled. "I have sent for tea. It should be here any moment. I shall not ask you where you went. It is possible I prefer not to know."

Jemima drew in her breath to say something, and no sensible answer occurred to her. She was saved from silence by the arrival of the maid with a heavy tray of tea, milk, hot water, and two plates of food: one of delicate savory sandwiches cut as fine as any she had seen in the high society of London; the other of little cakes of several sorts, some filled with whipped cream.

Celia thanked the maid and dismissed her, then without asking poured the tea for each of them.

Jemima accepted a sandwich, for the sake of good manners, and found it delicious. This whole performance was absurd, yet there was nothing remotely funny about it.

"I still can't believe Maria is gone," Celia said conversationally. "I was very fond of her."

"People speak well of her," Jemima replied. She wondered if Celia would tell her anything more about Maria, if she asked. Yet she could not work out if the woman had been completely honest with her or was playing some game of her own. Looking at her thin, intelligent face, with its almost hidden humor, she had an urgent feeling that it was the latter. But what was at the heart of it? Fear of losing her position in the Albright mansion? Jemima loved her brother, Daniel, but she had no intention whatever of being beholden to him for the rest of her life.

Celia was nodding. "They would do. She had a considerable charm."

What did that mean? Was "charm" a way of saying Maria was manipulative? Even dishonest?

"Did you know her well?" Jemima asked. What had she to lose? The police were going to charge her if they didn't have anyone else, no matter what Patrick did.

"I believed so," Celia answered. Now she was smiling sadly, her thoughts clearly turned inward.

Jemima could not afford diplomacy. "But you had cause to reverse your opinion?"

Celia gave a slight shrug of her thin shoulders. "I was surprised that she abandoned her husband and child. But I never had the opportunity to ask her why. How well does one ever know another person? You have to love without knowing, don't you think?" She looked at Jemima very directly, her gaze probing. "There are always things that are private, and should remain so." She was waiting for a reply.

"Yes, I suppose there are," Jemima agreed.

"When you are older, you will have secrets," Celia promised her. "That is one of the great burdens of a public life. Too many people know too much. One lives like a fish in an ornamental bowl."

"Goldfish . . ." Jemima was struggling to understand the obliqueness of the conversation. She took another sandwich to give herself time to think.

Celia moved the plate a little nearer her.

"It is the great drawback to political office, I think," she remarked.

Jemima was lost. "Political office? Has that something to do with Maria Cardew's death?"

Celia's eyes widened. "Oh my goodness, I hope not. I was merely making conversation. I wish I could offer you greater comfort. You came all this way from your own family, and now you seem to be caught up in our troubles, and I confess, I see no way out for you."

Jemima felt the panic well up inside her. She was stupid to have imagined Celia was going to be any help. The poor woman was facing the end of her own manner of living.

Jemima controlled herself with an effort. "I did not know Mrs. Cardew," she said levelly. "And she was already dead when I found her."

"Poor Maria," Celia murmured, pain quite naked in her voice. "She always struggled, but mostly for other people."

Jemima leaned forward. "Other people? What do you mean?"

"So very idealistic," Celia said,

not looking at Jemima but at some indefinable point on the far wall.

"What kind of ideals?" Maybe if she pressed hard enough, Celia might tell her something useful. "It sounds like she was . . . admirable. Could she have angered someone, do you think? One person's ideals sometimes endanger someone else's privileges." She was grasping desperately at straws.

"Oh, indeed," Celia said heavily. "Harley, for example, would not agree with her ideals. But of course he was not yet born when she was fighting her big battles."

"What battles?" Jemima said a little huskily. Was this something real at last?

"Thirty years ago." Celia avoided

Jemima's eyes.

Jemima's heart sank. For a moment she had felt hope surge up.

"Freedom for the slaves," Celia continued. "Real freedom, not just on a piece of paper. Even in the seventies and early eighties it was very hard for them. There was so much bitterness here in New York. Never knew what it was like farther south, except that it was so much worse."

"But surely Maria didn't ever have slaves!" Jemima protested.

"Oh, no, of course not," Celia agreed. "But she fought on their behalf. Ran herself into quite a lot of danger. I don't know a great deal about it, because my father was always very stern over such things.

Just as my brother is, and Harley, of course. But you'll know that because of his political stance."

"Political?" Jemima was lost again.

"Oh! Has he not told you?" Celia seemed surprised. "Harley is expecting that President Roosevelt will appoint him, as soon as he starts his second term in the new year. I'm sure you know he won the election last month."

"Really? I had no idea."

Celia met her eyes, no amusement or deceit in them.

"Oh, yes, very really indeed. Never doubt it."

"How . . . interesting," Jemima murmured, her mind racing. Could this possibly have anything to do with Maria's death? Was Celia trying to tell her this so obliquely that she could deny it later? Why? What did she know? Or was she deliberately leading Jemima astray?

She cleared her throat. "Do you think Mrs. Cardew's opinions were too radical?"

"I?" Celia said with surprise. "No. I admired her for them, as much as I understood what she was doing. I knew that it was dangerous for her." She hesitated so long Jemima thought she was not going to continue. Then suddenly she spoke again. "And I despised myself for not taking the same risks."

"What exactly was she doing?" Jemima was perfectly aware that the question was intrusive, but she had to try.

"Helping black people in trouble to escape the consequences of raising their voices, trying to be like white people, own property, have opinions," Celia said. "After the end of the Civil War, the resistance against change was too strong. The old attitudes were still everywhere."

"She must have been very brave," Jemima said with awe.

"And foolish," Celia added. "I liked her for it."

"But Mr. Albright didn't?"

"I really don't know how much he knew," Celia answered, her voice lifting in surprise as if she had only just realized the fact.

"And Harley?"

Celia smiled. "Certainly not. He

would be appalled. All he knew, all he knows, is that she had a certain reputation. Why don't you try the cakes? They are one of Cook's specialties."

Jemima recognized that the discussion was closed. She took one of the cakes, and it was indeed delicious.

Dinner was long and wretched. Phinnie chattered about her wedding, and never once looked at Jemima. Harley talked about politics, while Brent looked alternately happy and miserable. Mr. Albright spoke to Celia about people Jemima did not know.

Jemima felt awkward remaining downstairs after dinner was finished and they had all retired to the sitting room.

Phinnie sat close to Brent, as if she could not bear to have more distance between them than was necessary.

Mr. Albright sat in the largest armchair. Jemima imagined the very shape of it had molded itself to his body. Perhaps his father had sat in it before him, and his grand-father also. In time it would be Harley's, who now stood by the mantelpiece, too restless to sit down.

Jemima took one of the smaller chairs, but after only a few minutes she rose to her feet again. Maybe she was running away, but she found she would rather have stood outside in the snow in silence with Patrick Flannery than sit in this warm, lovely room with the Albrights and their stilted conversation.

"It has been a long and interesting day," she said to Mr. Albright. "Will you excuse me if I retire a little early?"

"An excellent idea," Harley replied before his father could. "Good night, Miss Pitt." There was no warmth in his voice.

"Good night, Miss Pitt," Celia echoed. "Sleep well."

Jemima acknowledged the good wishes, then turned and walked out the door, across the huge hall, and up the stairs. She had just reached the landing when she became aware of someone behind her. She turned quickly and saw Phinnie a couple of yards away from her.

"You've been asking about my mother," she accused, her voice harsh and bitter. "What are you trying to do? The police have been asking me questions, as if they thought I might have asked you to kill her, even paid you to do it!"

Jemima was stung by the injustice of it. "That's their job," she retorted sharply. "They are bound to realize I didn't do it. Why on earth would I?"

"For me, of course," Phinnie responded.

Jemima was stunned. "Don't be ridiculous! Apart from the fact that we have known each other only a

short while, why would I do anything so terrible?"

"So that when I marry Brent I
can pay you, of course!" Phinnie
replied. "Either with money or by
making sure you meet all the right
people in New York. You are clever
enough to have thought of that."

"Oh, yes!" Jemima agreed. "And
even blackmail you for the rest of
your life?"

Phinnie gasped, her face going
pale. "You would, wouldn't you?"

"Well, I suppose if I'd killed poor
Maria to stop her from bursting
into your wedding and spoiling it, I
would probably stoop to pretty
much anything," Jemima said cut-
tingly, with an anger close to de-
spair. "But as I already told you, all

I wanted to do was help *Harley* find her so that *he* could pay her to stay away. He was afraid she might make a scene and embarrass everyone, ruin the family's reputation. And you never know, when the president comes to consider him for high office, he might think you an inappropriate relative for a man in the public eye." She knew the last bit would hurt Phinnie, and she meant it to. Phinnie had been willing enough to hurt her.

"So you . . . you didn't . . ." Phinnie said slowly, the angry color draining out of her face leaving her sickly pale.

"No, *of course* I didn't!" Jemima snapped. She was about to turn away and go on to her bedroom when she realized that Phinnie's amazement and relief were real. She had truly feared Jemima had killed her mother. "I saw Maria once, for a moment, in Central Park," she said gently. "When we were following her, and she turned to look back at the snow on the trees. There was such joy on her face at the beauty of them that for a moment she too was beautiful. The next time I saw her she was dead."

Phinnie's eyes filled with tears. "I don't want to like her," she whispered. "She left me! It took me all my life, until I met Brent, to stop wanting her to come back and explain to me what was more important to her than staying with me."

Jemima wanted to put her arms around Phinnie, be — for an instant at least — the sister she did not have. But it was too soon.

"That is what I am trying to find out," she said instead. "I'll start again tomorrow morning. I promise."

Phinnie nodded, too close to losing control to speak.

The next day was bitter. The wind cut like the edge of a knife, and there was ice in the breath of it.

Jemima would rather have stayed inside, but she had very little time left. The memory of the prison always hovered at the edges of her mind like an encroaching darkness.

Was it time she sent a telegram to her father and asked him to come? But what could he do here anyway?

Because of course he would come, and he'd find a way to learn the truth and prove it. But part of her didn't want to send for him. Part of her wanted to find out what happened without his help. Was she just being foolish?

She increased her pace, footsteps crunching in the snow. A woman passed her on the pavement, walking briskly, bent forward and huddled into her coat. The man a few steps behind her had his hat jammed on his head and his scarf over half his face.

An automobile passed them all, the driver sitting up rigidly, having difficulty keeping the snow from coating the glass windshield. She smiled to herself, happy to be walking.

At last she reached the coffee shop, her hands so numb she could hardly grasp the door handle. A man opened it for her and she thanked him. Inside she looked around for Patrick. When she saw him, her heart lifted and she found herself smiling as he stood up and came over to her.

"Are you all right?" he said anxiously. "I wish you didn't have to be out today . . ."

"There isn't time," she said simply. "And I have a lot to tell you."

He guided her to the seat where he had been waiting, putting his arm around her shoulders. Even a day ago she would have moved away. Today she let it be. It was comfortable and she was willing to admit it. He held the chair for her, then ordered hot coffee, and more for himself.

Warming her hands on the mug, the chatter of all manner of languages around her, she told him what Celia had said about Harley and his ambitions, about Maria Cardew and her rescue of former slaves in trouble, and then Phinnie's accusation that Jemima had killed Maria — and finally, her belief that Jemima hadn't done it.

"So that makes you sure she wasn't the one who killed Maria?" he said. There was no time to be less than frank.

"Yes, I am. She truly believed I had done it, which means she couldn't have. We need to learn more about that part of her life. But if Maria risked her life helping black people who used to be slaves, she will have made enemies."

He smiled with wry, sad humor. "I know it's 1904, but not everything has changed. Old wounds are slow to heal. We're said to be 'a melting pot,' but there's a lot that hasn't melted yet. Did Celia say anything about Sara Godwin?"

"No. Patrick . . ." A thought occurred to her, and although she hated it, it had to be voiced. "Do you think Sara Godwin could have killed her? Perhaps Maria's death had nothing to do with the Albrights or her past at all but was because of an enmity between the two women?"

There was regret in his face. "It could even be that whoever killed her mistook her for Sara Godwin. I've been asking around more to find anyone who knew them a bit better, and another woman in the same building said they were always very careful, as if they were constantly afraid of something. According to Ellie, Maria said Sara thought someone had been following her, and she was afraid that he knew where she lived. But we have no description of him."

"He could be anyone," she said, a wave of hopelessness overwhelming her. "How can we even look for him?"

Patrick reached across the table and put his hand over hers, holding her when she tried to pull away. She stopped pulling. His touch was warm and strong.

"I don't need to find him to prove he existed," he told her. "Two witnesses, independent of each other, and a little more about her past, will be enough to prove he could have killed her. We just have to know what kind of woman she was, and make a case for why it is believable that he mistook Maria for her. They did look alike. That much I know already, from questioning their neighbors."

"Will it be enough?" she said

anxiously. "Won't they still think it's me, because I was there and we don't know anything about this man?"

"I won't let them think that," he promised.

She looked away. Suddenly it mattered more that he believed her, that he did not for a moment think she was guilty, than that she still might face trial for murder and not be able to prove her innocence.

He interrupted her thoughts. "Finish your coffee. We have a lot to do." He said it gently, but it was an instruction, almost an order.

Toward the end of the day they met with an old man, nearly blind, who said he had known Sara well. He had been a cobbler. He knew everyone's feet.

Jemima and Patrick sat with him in his small tenement room sharing hot food that Patrick had bought from a shop in the narrow street opposite. It was very savory meat cooked and then wrapped in leaves. Patrick told her the shop owners were Russian immigrants and they had told him the name of the dish, but he couldn't now pronounce it. It was delicious, though, and Jemima told him so.

The cobbler also ate his with relish.

"Sara," he said with a smile of memory. "Good feet, she had. But sickly, even then."

"Even then?" Patrick said quickly. "How long ago was that?"

"Oh, thirty years or so. Had a hard time, Sara did. Wonder she lived so long." He blinked several times, as if to hide tears. "Wouldn't have made it without Maria."

Jemima leaned forward quickly. "I thought that thirty years ago Maria was busy helping people fight against injustice? Is that not true?"

The cobbler stared at her, a touch of anger in his eyes. "Course she did! Both of them. That's when it all happened. In the seventies, before they came to this part of the city."

Patrick started to speak, then stopped. He nodded to Jemima.

"If you knew them, then I'd really like to hear the truth," Jemima said. "Her daughter is my friend and I think she deserves to hear something more than gossip, a lot of which is unkind."

"Unkind!" the cobbler snorted. It was dim inside the small room. He burned a stove to keep the air from freezing but he clearly could not afford to burn a light as well, and the window was blurring over with snow. "That what you call it? Bastards deserve to be hanged themselves."

Jemima waited. She did not even dare glance at Patrick, but she was acutely aware of his presence in the room, sitting opposite her, their knees almost touching.

"Them as used to be slaves got into a bit of trouble back then," the cobbler began. "Blacks, you know?

Some folks were fine, but in some ways it seemed we weren't so very far from the South. The ones who'd run away were here and there. Some folks didn't think they should own things, like horses and land and such. You know?" He looked at Patrick, his eyebrows raised in question. He had caught Jemima's English accent and clearly did not expect her to understand.

"I've heard," Patrick said, nodding. He was Irish; he knew about discrimination.

"Sara used to help people," the cobbler went on. "Got into it with Maria. There was one real bad time. Black man been a slave, owned a real nice place. Some folks got very upset about it. Spread around stories that he'd stole it, that they should turn him out of it. It turned into a big fight on the street. Women and children in it too. Sara and Maria were both there. Feller who used to be a slave fought to get the women out. In the end, one man was killed. Son of a bitch had it coming. He had no regard for the safety of the women or the children, injured a few in that fight. But he was white. Maria fell in love with the man what did it. Married him, she did. Some folks never forgave her for that."

"That was the scandal?" Jemima asked. She didn't know what to make of this information. How could Maria have been married once before? Did the Albrights know about it? Her heart was racing.

"It's enough," the cobbler replied, pursing his lips. "Black don't marry white. Some folks consider it unnatural, a sin against God, like."

"Where is that man now?" Jemima forced herself to ask, and yet she dreaded the answer. Maria had lived in an apartment with Sara Godwin. Had she had a falling out with this other man? Could he have done it?

"Don't know," the cobbler replied with a sniff. "He was taken down here in New York, to be tried for killing that white son of a bitch. Pardon my language, miss."

Jemima shivered at the word "tried." She felt Patrick's knees touch hers, just for a moment. Had he meant to, or was he just moving because he was stiff?

"What happened?" she whispered.

"They told her he died in prison," the cobbler replied, his voice hoarse. "But I heard after that he hadn't. Don't know what was true."

"What happened to Maria?" Patrick asked.

"Some rich white feller kind of looked after her. She were a real handsome woman. His name was All-something . . ."

"Albright?" Jemima filled in.

"Yes, something like that. He was married, of course. Men like that always are. Got to keep the family going. Anyway, she married his business partner, or something. English . . . like you," he said to Jemima. "Is that why you're asking all this?"

"Yes. Maria's daughter is my friend."

"Well, ain't it a small world. And this daughter come here just as poor Maria's killed? That's a terrible shame. You tell her that her mother was one of the best ladies that ever drew breath, you hear me?"

"Yes," Jemima answered. "Yes, I will. I promise."

Outside again in the more heavily falling snow, Jemima turned to Patrick. He was standing to the windward of her, sheltering her from the worst of it. It blew against him and piled on his shoulders.

"Do you think someone killed her because years ago she married a black man who used to be a slave?" she asked.

"I think that's very possible, though it's a shame that it is," he replied. "Are you prepared for Delphinia to learn this?"

"No!" She looked away from him, down at the snow around her boots. "No. She might not mind, but imagine what the Albrights would make of it if they don't already know!"

"Delphinia's a Cardew," he pointed out. "Come out of the snow. We can find somewhere better than this to talk." He took her arm as he said it, gently but too firmly for her to resist.

Jemima said nothing. It was difficult to talk out here in the street because the wind snatched her words and the freezing air almost choked her.

They walked side by side until they came to an alley and found room to stand in a recessed doorway, sheltered from the worst of the weather.

She remembered Harley Albright's words to her, before they had even found Maria's body, when it was still a matter of stopping her from creating a scene at the wedding.

"Marguerite Albright, Harley's mother," she began. "He said to me that she had told him about Maria and what a terrible woman she was."

"Well, if the cobbler is right, then Mr. Albright was very fond of Maria, and Mrs. Albright was probably jealous," he pointed out.

"Do you suppose she knew about Maria's first husband?"

"It's definitely possible. What are you thinking, Jemima? That it was one of the Albrights after all?"

He was worried, she could see. It would be difficult to prove; might his superiors try to prevent him from even suggesting it? Jemima would be a much easier target, much more comfortable. Nobody in New York would care if she was convicted. Would it matter to them that her father was important in England? The fear came back over her like an icy wave.

Patrick saw it in her eyes. "Jemima, don't! I won't let that happen," he promised.

"You might not be able to stop it," she replied. "If Mrs. Albright knew the truth about Maria, then she would've cared very much indeed that Phinnie didn't marry into the Albright family."

"Then why wouldn't she just tell Brent the truth?" he asked."

"Maybe she died before she had the chance? Or Brent doesn't care as much?" Another thought occurred to her. "What if . . . what if Marguerite Albright had written to Maria back when she was in England and told her that her first husband was alive after all? Then she was not a widow! She was a bigamist! Her marriage to Edward Cardew was not legal."

He was watching her closely, trying to read what she was thinking now.

"Phinnie would be illegitimate," she told him. "Would she still be Cardew's heir?"

"She's still his daughter!" He was angry at the injustice and it was naked in his face. "Maria thought she was a widow. In fact, we don't know for certain that she wasn't. Mrs. Albright could have said her husband was alive simply out of . . ." He stopped.

"Out of spite?" Jemima finished.

"Revenge, for Mr. Albright having liked Maria so much?"

He shook his head, his eyes very grave. "Not just that. More importantly, so the company's power and money will stay with the Albright family."

"But she died well before Brent proposed marriage to Phinnie . . . oh." Now it was there, real and cold as ice. "She told Harley. Of course. And if Brent married Phinnie, then between the two of them they would own three-quarters of the company: Phinnie's entire Cardew share from her father, and Brent's half of the Albright share." She leaned forward and put her hands over her face, pushing her fingers through her hair, heedless of the mess she made of it. "Poor Phinnie."

Patrick said nothing. He understood too well to say something meaningless.

"She's so much in love with him," Jemima went on. "Do you think he is even half as much in love with her?" She did not look up at him. She was afraid he was going to struggle to find some comfortable half-truth.

"No," he said softly. "If you really love someone you stick by them, no matter what. You don't doubt them, or make a way to get out of it."

Now she did look up. "What makes you say that? Did he make a way to get out of it?"

"Yes. When I questioned him, he didn't defend her — not completely. If anyone said that about you, I would have defended you, whether I had the right to or not."

She tried to smile through the emotion that was beating so hard inside her it almost robbed her of breath.

"Thanks to Harley they *are* saying it about me," she pointed out. "He tricked me well. He spent enough time with me to guess I would get impatient and leave the coffee shop. He must've also sent the young boy to tell me the room number. I'm sure he had a backup plan, but he didn't need one. I played right into his hands." Jemima's voice was bitter.

"I know what people are saying thanks to Harley." Now his eyes hid nothing. "And I am defending you. I'll prove you didn't do it. We're nearly there now. But you can't help Delphinia, except maybe to make her see the truth about the Albrights, and to give her the knowledge that her mother was a good woman who got caught up in a tragedy that wasn't of her making."

"Why did she leave Phinnie? She was only two years old!" Jemima protested.

"What if Mrs. Albright didn't write to Maria, as we supposed, but to Cardew, telling him all about Maria's first marriage? Cardew may have given Maria no choice.

271

And she certainly wouldn't be allowed to take Phinnie with her, even if she had the means to look after her. But he must've loved Phinnie enough to leave it at that, at least."

"I suppose I should have known that," she said. "It explains everything, doesn't it?"

"Except what happened to Sara Godwin," Patrick agreed.

"Why did she run off, and where is she now? Hadn't she enough loyalty to see that Maria at least had a decent burial?" Jemima asked, somewhat angry.

"Perhaps she is afraid they'll come after her too?" Patrick said.

Jemima tried to imagine the conflict in Sara Godwin. She owed

Maria her life, but she was ill, alone now, and knew that Maria had been murdered. Perhaps she even knew who had done it. And the woman in the same building had said Sara had been followed . . .

Patrick must have been thinking the same thing.

"We must find her," he said with sudden urgency. "If she saw the man following her, she might know who it was, or at least be able to describe him. I suspect that it was Harley, though. I think he killed Maria and then very neatly organized it so you would be the one to find her. But we need to prove that."

Jemima nodded hesitantly. "Yes."

"What is it?" he asked. "Why

don't you want to? Are you afraid we're wrong?" He put his hand over hers. "Jemima, we aren't wrong. It all fits together and makes sense of all the bits we couldn't understand before."

She met his eyes. "I know. I just hate that Sara owed so much to Maria but just ran away when she was dead, instead of staying to help. I understand! Maybe I wouldn't have done better. But I still hate it."

"I'll find her alone, then," he answered.

She glared at him. "No, you won't! I'm coming with you."

This time he laughed, his face eased in relief. She realized that it very much mattered to him that she came, and the feeling was wonderful, as if the cold outside barely existed. She withdrew her hand from his. "Let's begin."

It took them all that day, and the next. It was almost Christmas when, after much questioning, pleading, and even promises, they finally climbed the rickety stairs in the tenement building where Sara Godwin had supposedly taken refuge. They had found her largely by trailing her attempts to earn money by taking small jobs, never staying in one dwelling more than two days at most, as if she was afraid that someone was pursuing her.

The snow had eased and the east wind had dropped when finally, feet aching and bones cold, they knocked on the door of the smallest apartment on the top floor.

The door opened tentatively and a woman looked out, keeping her weight behind the door so she could close it if needed. Her face was filled with alarm.

Jemima recognized her immediately. It was the same woman who had been walking in Central Park and had turned back to gaze up at the snow-laden branches with such joy. Suddenly she understood. "Maria?" Jemima said gently.

The woman's face filled with terror and she tried to push the door closed.

Patrick leaned his weight against it, forcing it to stay open.

"I'm Jemima Pitt," Jemima said gently. "I'm Phinnie's friend. I've come over from England to be with her for her wedding. I understand that you can't be . . . and why."

Tenderness and grief filled the woman's eyes. She must have been over fifty, and had certainly not had an easy life, but she was still beautiful.

"You don't know why," she said quietly. "I . . . I wish I could . . ."

"I do know," Jemima said, contradicting her. "Mrs. Albright wrote to Mr. Cardew and told him about your first husband. You had no choice."

Maria's grief was impossible to hide. She pulled the door open and Jemima and Patrick went inside.

The room was tiny and the air was chill, but it was clean and there was a feeling of hominess to it because of the few personal belongings scattered about: There were embroidered pillow covers on the narrow bed, half a dozen books on a shelf, and a photograph of a handsome black man, smiling, on the bedside table.

"I never stopped thinking about her," Maria said as Patrick closed the door. "But I couldn't even see her. It would have spoiled things for her. Why have you come here?"

Jemima hesitated, and it was Patrick who answered.

"Because they are blaming Jemima for killing you, either with Phinnie's help, or at the least for her sake."

Maria paled. "Why? That's . . ." Then she understood. "It was Harley, wasn't it?" She closed her eyes, and for a moment she swayed a little, as if she might fall.

Patrick took hold of her, supporting part of her weight, and eased her to the one moderately comfortable chair in the room.

She waited a moment, then opened her eyes. "Sara was dying," she said with difficulty, her voice thick with tears. "She tricked me. She sent me on an errand to help someone, and she took my place. She wore my clothes — we were always the same size — and I suppose we look a bit alike. Harley hadn't seen me for years."

"It wouldn't matter if he had, and knew he was wrong," Patrick pointed out. "He identified the body as yours, so it served his purpose well enough. You weren't going to come forward and say he was wrong."

"I couldn't! Not without Phinnie learning all about me, and that she was illegitimate." She said the word as if it hurt her. "Even though I thought Joe was dead at the time. Of course I would never have married Albert and left America if I'd known he was still alive!"

"And Phinnie's wedding?" Jemima asked.

"I just wanted to see her. I wouldn't have spoken to her, just watched. There'll be a crowd. No one would have seen me."

"And Sara Godwin?" This time it was Patrick who asked the question.

"There was no one else to look after her properly. No matter what, I couldn't leave her to die alone — and yet that's just what I did!"

"She chose to." Jemima shook her head. "She did that for you, perhaps to thank you for all you'd done for her."

"I've got to bury her properly. They're not putting her in a pauper's grave. I've got nearly enough money." She looked from Jemima to Patrick. "Whatever you think of me, please see that that happens?"

"We will," Patrick promised instantly. "But before that, we have to make sure we have the evidence to prove it was Harley Albright who killed Sara, whether he thought she was you or not."

"How are you going to do that?" Maria asked doubtfully.

Patrick smiled at her. "You're coming to the police station and you'll tell my bosses the whole story, including that Harley was following you a day or so before Sara was killed. We all know he identified her as you. We know that Phinnie is Mr. Cardew's heir, and that when she marries Brent he will become heir to three-quarters of the Albright and Cardew business. The only way for Harley to keep his power and fortune is to discredit Phinnie, either so Brent doesn't marry her and the shares stay equal among the three of them — or, better still, so that she is written off as illegitimate, Mr. Cardew has no heirs, and the power reverts to the Albrights."

"Poor Harley," Maria said with regret. "He was a nice child. So handsome, with all that fair hair. Marguerite adored him. One loves one's children . . . so much."

"When this is settled, will you meet Phinnie?" Jemima asked urgently.

"Oh, no. I won't spoil her happiness. It will be terribly hard for Brent to come to terms with his brother's crime. He will need her support. And Celia will help. She was always strong . . . and loyal, as much as they would allow."

Jemima glanced at Patrick and saw him nod very slightly. Did he really know her so well he understood what she was asking? She realized that the joy that Maria was alive, and the relief that she herself would be cleared of any suspicion, was suddenly horribly overshadowed by the thought of leaving New York after the wedding . . . if it proceeded! She might never see Patrick again, and that hurt more than she had thought possible.

Her own mother had come from a very good family, and scandalized them all by marrying a policeman at a time when policemen were socially regarded as little better than bailiffs or dustmen. Early in their marriage times had been hard and money scarce, but she had been, and still was, extraordinarily happy. And unlike so many women, she had never been bored . . . or lonely.

This was ridiculous! Yes, she admitted to herself, she was in love with Patrick Flannery, very much in love. But he had not mentioned marriage, and had probably not given it a thought!

Jemima looked at Maria, and read in the older woman's eyes an understanding so complete that it made the color burn up Jemima's cheeks. But then, Maria had married the man she loved, in spite of the fact that he was black, and had once been owned, like an animal.

It had not stopped her.

"Brent might not marry Phinnie," Jemima said aloud. "She deserves someone who loves her wholeheartedly, whoever her mother is and whatever the circumstances. You don't become a different person just because you discover something about your birth. And money is nice, but it has nothing to do with real happiness. You and I both know that." It was a challenge, and she wanted an answer.

Maria smiled and touched Jemima's hand lightly. "Of course we do. Although hunger is hard, perhaps harder than you know."

"Isn't hunger of the heart because you denied yourself even harder?" Jemima asked.

"I don't know, because I was always rash enough not to try it," Maria answered. "And it cost me dear . . . but I never doubted it was worth it."

Two days later, Harley was arrested. Brent postponed indefinitely his marriage to Phinnie. It was a polite fiction. Everyone knew that it would never take place. Celia stepped forward to comfort her family and support them, especially Rothwell, as she had done discreetly all their lives.

Phinnie and Jemima left the Albright house and took lodgings in the city, until they should find passage home, early in the New Year. Phinnie's means were more than sufficient to look after all their needs.

Early on Christmas morning, Jemima persuaded Phinnie to meet Maria.

It was awkward at first.

"I don't wish to," Phinnie said miserably. "I don't know what to say!"

"Start with 'Hello,' " Jemima replied. "I know everything fell apart and nothing was the way you hoped it would be, but don't let go of what is good. You have plenty of time to meet someone who loves you, no matter who your family is or what's happened."

"I thought Brent loved me . . ."

"I know. And maybe he thought so too," Jemima said. "But none of that has anything to do with meeting Maria. Come on."

Reluctantly, Phinnie agreed. They put on their best winter coats and hats and walked down to Central Park, to the place where Harley and Jemima had seen Maria turn back to gaze at the snow-laden trees. They were edged with snow again today, glittering white for Christmas.

"There," Jemima pointed. Fifty yards ahead of them she saw Patrick. It took her a moment to be certain it was him: He was wearing not his police uniform but a plain dark overcoat, and he was bareheaded. Beside him was Maria, looking at them as if she had known them even in the farthest distance.

She took a tentative step forward, then another.

"I'm frightened," Phinnie whispered to Jemima. "What if she doesn't like me?"

"She loves you!" Jemima replied. "She always did. Come on!" She stepped out, taking Phinnie by the arm and pulling her forward.

There were other people on the path as well, but none of them took any notice. It was only as they came much closer that Jemima realized that the black man a little behind Maria was the same man she had seen in the photograph beside Maria's bed. He was older, grayer at the temples, but the smile had not changed, nor the curious mixture of shyness and inner confidence on display in the picture.

Phinnie stopped in front of Maria. They were the same height, and had the same soft features and dark eyes, the same grace of movement.

Maria held out her hands. Slowly Phinnie took them and held on.

When Jemima looked at Patrick she knew that it was going to be all right. She forgot about Phinnie and Maria, even about the man, Joe, whom Maria introduced quietly and with pride.

"I think you took care of Phinnie's happiness," Patrick said, taking Jemima's arm and beginning to walk toward the edge of the path.

"But what about us?" he asked, stopping and turning to face her. "Are we going to be all right too?"

She looked up at him. She was almost certain of what he meant. It was there in his eyes, his whole face, but she needed to hear him say it.

"I don't know," she answered. "Are we?"

"I will be, if you marry me. Will you?"

"I think I probably will."

He looked startled. "What?"

Jemima laughed and reached up to touch his cheek with her gloved fingers. "I will marry you, and I think I will probably be all right, for always."

He leaned forward and kissed her.

The passersby smiled, and in the distance Christmas bells began to ring.

ABOUT THE AUTHOR

Anne Perry is the bestselling author of eleven earlier holiday novels — *A Christmas Journey, A Christmas Visitor, A Christmas Guest, A Christmas Secret, A Christmas Beginning, A Christmas Grace, A Christmas Promise, A Christmas Odyssey, A Christmas Homecoming, A Christmas Garland,* and *A Christmas Hope* — as well as the bestselling William Monk series, the bestselling Charlotte and Thomas Pitt series, and five World War I novels. She lives in

Scotland.

www.anneperry.co.uk

Anne Perry is available for select readings and lectures. To inquire about a possible appearance, please contact the Penguin Random House Speakers Bureau at 212-572-2013 or speakers @penguinrandomhouse.com.